CANADA'S HAUNTED COAST

True Ghost Stories of the Maritimes

D1636060

Vernon Oickle

GHOST HOUSE

Ghost House Books

© 2008 by Lone Pine Publishing International Inc.
First printed in 2008 10 9 8 7 6 5 4 3 2 1
Printed in Canada

The Publisher: Lone Pine Publishing International
Distributed by Lone Pine Publishing
10145–81 Avenue
Edmonton, AB Canada, T6E 1W9

Websites: www.lonepinepublishing.com
www.ghostbooks.net

Library and Archives Canada Cataloguing in Publication

Oickle, Vernon L.
Canada's Haunted Coast : True ghost stories of the maritimes / Vernon Oickle.

ISBN-13: 978-1-55105-598-5
ISBN-10: 1-55105-598-8

1. Ghosts--Maritime Provinces. 2. Legends--Maritime Provinces. I. Title.

GR113.5.M37O323 2008   398.209715'05   C2008-901749-8

Editorial Director: Nancy Foulds
Project Editor: Sheila Quinlan
Production Manager: Gene Longson
Layout and Production: Megan Fischer, Michael Cooke
Cover Design: Gerry Dotto

Photo Credits: Every effort has been made to accurately credit photographers. Any errors
or omissions should be directed to the publisher for changes in future editions. The photographs and illustrations in this book are reproduced with the kind permission of the
following sources: Bryan Harn: 42; Fred Hatfield: 46; Robert Hirtle: 168; Linda Layton:
171; Vernon Oickle: 11, 13, 31, 32, 35, 38, 91, 93, 120, 163; Chris Reardon: 110, 112; Hal
Thompson: 59; White Point Beach Lodge: 22.

PC: P5

In memory of my dearly departed father,
Lloyd, and father-in-law, Ike.
May your spirits live on forever.

CONTENTS

Chapter Four: Less Ghostly (But Still Mysterious) Local Legends

Chapter Five: Premonitions, Forerunners and Messages from Beyond

Acknowledgements

Shortly after *Ghost Stories of the Maritimes Vol. II* was published in 2001, I immediately discovered there were still many more good stories that I had not included in either of the first two books. Over the next few years, I continued to collect stories that I hoped would someday find their way into a third volume in this series. Thankfully, in 2006, Lone Pine agreed that, based on the success of the previous two collections, it was time for another instalment, and the work began.

Producing these books is a major commitment, but it is one I embrace with much enthusiasm. It goes without saying that such a project is a great deal of work, and these books could not happen without the generous support of many people, particularly the storytellers. To start with, then, I must acknowledge the many people who shared their experiences and who are included within the pages of the book you are about to read. They include Bill and Donna Alsop, Shawn Baker, Bob Benson, Dave Conrad, Pam Foley, Florence Godin, David Goss, Andrew Hebda, Danny Hennigar, Noreen Hirtle, Patrick Hirtle, Robert Hirtle, Linda Layton, Joan LeBlanc, Lucy MacIntosh, Bessie MacKenzie, Lynn MacLean, Allan MacRae, Dianne Marshall, Nancy Oulton, Wendy Patterson, Don Roberts, Ian Ross, Andy Smith, Hal Thompson, Julie Wamboldt, the staff and management of White Point Beach Resort, and those people who shared their stories but asked that their identities be protected. A special note of thanks to those who assisted with photos, including Bryan Harn, Fred Hatfield and Danny Morton.

I also want to thank Nancy Foulds and her team at Lone Pine Publishing for believing that I could do it one more time, and with their support, here it is. They are a fantastic group of people to work with, and I hope our affiliation will continue and that we will someday work together again on another project.

Lastly, I would be terribly remiss if I did not thank my greatest supporters, who have given me the time and inspiration to see this project through to its reality. Of course I'm talking about my wife, Nancy, and our sons, Kellen and Colby. It takes a great deal of time and energy to research, tabulate and write a book of this nature, and that means I've had to take myself away from them to make this happen. But they've understood, and they've given me their blessing.

I hope you enjoy reading this collection of stories as much as I have enjoyed putting it together, and I thank you for believing in the unbelievable. Happy haunting.

Introduction

Growing up in rural Nova Scotia, I became accustomed to many old superstitions and beliefs that seem to permeate every nuance of this region of Canada. In this part of the country, it's not uncommon to hear people speak of forerunners, premonitions and other folklore as if they were fact. As a child, one tends to hang on to these things, and that is exactly what I did. Years later, when I became a journalist, I decided to research and collect these stories with hopes that someday they would become a book. What you are holding is the result of that effort.

I consider myself fortunate to have grown up and now to reside in this part of the country, where my wife and I are raising our two sons. It is the people that make this place special. I love living here, and I am overwhelmed that I have been given this tremendous opportunity to write these books. It is not a responsibility I take lightly. This is the third volume in a series of books on Maritime ghost stories that I have produced for Lone Pine. The experience of collecting the data and writing the stories has been most rewarding and personally fulfilling. I hope you enjoy reading them as much as I enjoy telling them.

I hold a tremendous amount of respect for the people who have so generously related their stories to me, not only for this volume but for the previous two collections as well. There is no shortage of material in this region for such books. However, these projects would not be possible were it not for the people who graciously shared their experiences. Granted, on occasion, there are obstacles to convincing some people to tell their stories. They fear ridicule from those who may

1
Haunted Inns, Restaurants and Other Buildings

The Haunting of Henry House

Almost two centuries ago, William Alexander Henry, one of Nova Scotia's Fathers of Confederation and the mayor of Halifax in 1870, lived in the city's south end in a stately stone house once known as the Granite Brewery. At that time, the home's civic address was 50 Pleasant Street. Today, it is 1222 Barrington Street.

This historic property at 1222 Barrington Street in Halifax is said to be haunted by a variety of apparitions.

Henry was a lawyer, a legislator and a statesman. Born in Halifax, his family subsequently moved to Antigonish, Nova Scotia, where, at age 24, he became the youngest member of the House of Assembly. He frequently travelled to Halifax to attend the sessions of the legislature, and in 1854, his appointment as Attorney General most likely influenced his decision to purchase the stately home that, in time, became known as Henry House. From Halifax, Henry travelled to the Confederation conferences in Quebec and Charlottetown in 1863 and in London in 1866. At the London meeting, he was one of the two members in attendance who produced the original draft of the British North America Act, the legislation that led to the formation of this country we now call Canada.

The Halifax home was built of Scottish granite and ironstone in a side hall plan that is typical of a 19th-century townhouse. Ironstone and granite were used for many Halifax residences of the period. The ironstone was obtained locally, and the granite blocks were often imported from the Old Country as ballast in the holds of sailing ships. When Henry moved to Pleasant Street, a number of prominent merchants would have lived nearby, as well as on the streets opening from it in the south end, where fields were quickly developing into residential areas in the 1860s and 1870s. Halifax was beginning its transformation from a port community to the sprawling metro area it is today.

During his time in Halifax, Henry entertained many of the period's most influential businessmen, politicians, diplomats and community leaders at his beautiful manor, and among them were most likely those who played a prominent role in Confederation. Today, in that same Maritime tradition of welcome, Henry House is a popular restaurant and pub, serving fine food and thirst-quenching libations to satisfy any and all tastes. And by the accounts of many eye-witnesses, the establishment is also said to be haunted.

Current owners Bill and Donna Alsop became attracted to Henry House when they were looking to relocate to Nova Scotia from Ontario. Although the premises was never officially listed for sale by the previous owners, Donna says when they saw the house, they just knew they had to have it. It was exactly what they were looking for, she recalls. Following a series of successful negotiations, the Alsops purchased the business in 2002 and today operate it as a restaurant and pub. They are also very careful to maintain its heritage and architectural integrity, both of which Donna says attracted them to the property in the first place. However, she continues, if anyone had told her that the house was haunted, she might have had second thoughts about buying it, but then quickly adds, "I doubt it. It's like we were attracted to this place for some reason, and we love it here. I believe we were meant to be here."

Donna Alsop, the current owner of Henry House, has experienced several paranormal phenomena in the building, including one at this bar.

Although there are many stories that indicate the property did come with a few ghosts, she calls this place home. "Let's just say I was never a fan of scary movies," Donna says. "If you would have ever told me that I would be living in a building that someone actually thought had a spirit attached to it, I would have told you that it would never happen. I've been in houses before where it just doesn't feel right. You know, it's that little something that makes the tiny hairs on the back of your neck stand up. Sometimes it's like that in here, and it wasn't long after we bought the house that we began to hear stories that the place was haunted."

In talking with the staff, Donna and Bill soon found that many things had happened there in the past that might lead people to believe there are, indeed, ghosts in the house. "For starters, they told us stories of the beer taps being turned on by themselves, which just can't happen, but the story goes that one of the managers had been working in the kitchen one day, and when she turned away and then back again, all the beer taps suddenly came on all at once. There was no way they could come on by themselves because they were all hand pumps, so there could not have been any electrical glitch, if that's what you're thinking. These beer taps have to be turned on manually by hand. It's just these types of eerie experiences that make people think there are ghosts here, and it is a strange feeling."

And Donna says there are many similar stories. "Women who worked here wouldn't close up alone at night because there are parts of this place that just don't feel right. In particular, there was one room upstairs that had a weird feeling about it, so the staff totally avoided it. If anyone was closing up at night, they wanted to do it in twos and threes. It was this sort of thing that made us wonder if something really was going on around here."

Bill and Donna spoke with the previous owner, but he didn't believe in ghosts or anything like that, so he was never convinced that the place was haunted. "But I believe that some people are more open to supernatural events at different levels," Donna says. "I believe that people will experience things in a different way, that's why some people experience these phenomena and others do not."

When the Alsops purchased Henry House, they did so planning to live in the building, something no one had done for many years. "We had a plan to renovate and refurbish the fourth floor for our living quarters. That was the garret where the servants stayed at one time, particularly when the Henrys lived here. The stories were not disturbing enough for us to reconsider that plan. For sure, if we had heard something horrific had taken place in the house, we may have had second thoughts, but these stories were not like that. If something awful had occurred here, I would have had difficulty living here, but we didn't find any evidence of anything like that. We pushed ahead with our plans, but at the same time, I began to do some research into the building known as the Granite Brewery."

Donna discovered that one of the most popular stories of a ghost sighting connected with Henry House is that of seeing a female servant on the stairway located at the main entrance. Another one is of seeing a woman dressed in Victorian-era clothing outside the building in what would now be the driveway. Many people have reported seeing these two ghosts over the years. "There was one staff member who was scared by what had happened to him," Donna says.

"This staff member was working in what is now the bar area [the lower level] when he said he felt himself being tapped on the shoulder several times. He looked around, but there was no one else near him. He insists he was alone, but he says he has no doubt that someone tapped him. It was very distinct, and he's very convincing when he tells you about it. Clearly, something happened to him."

Shortly after purchasing the property, Donna and Bill were having some restoration work done on the front exterior of the house. They hoped to restore it to its original appearance, and they were using a local contractor who was well known for doing that type of work. His name was Hal. "He does amazing work. He looked at a picture of how the house appeared back in 1870, and he was able to make it look just like it did in that period," Donna explains.

But she quickly adds that the work wasn't without its unusual experiences. "As the guys who worked for Hal tore off the old wood, taking it back to the original porch that was there in the 1800s, they found a very old note folded up in among the debris. When they unfolded the note, they found two words on it. The note said, 'Hi Hal.' I kid you not. This guy and his crew insist that it was real, and I've seen the note. It looks pretty authentic to me."

Donna says Hal also reported talking to a female visitor he encountered one day while working on the side of the building. "He says he was talking to a woman one minute, then he claims she disappeared. Just like that, she was gone."

About a year later, Donna says a psychic who had been in Halifax promoting a book she had recently written came into Henry House. "I was sitting in the dining room by myself that night. This woman was from England, and I'm sure she didn't know the history of the building. She came in, sat at the bar and looked across the room. There was not another soul in the room, other than me of course. However, this woman said she could see so much activity in the room that it was overwhelming to her. She said there was so much supernatural activity that it was like a fog hanging over the room. She looked up the staircase and said there was a woman standing on the stairs. She described this woman as having long, dark hair and wearing a black dress with a white collar on it and said she was very upset because she had issues with her father that had not been resolved in her lifetime. This psychic was very articulate in her descriptions of what she was seeing."

Donna's husband, Bill, experienced something in one of the back rooms in the basement that today is used for a storage area. "On three different occasions the lights went out while he was in there, and it's very dark when the lights go out in that room. There is no way that light switch can go off on its own. It's just not possible, and to this day we cannot explain how that could have happened."

On another occasion, Donna was in the kitchen with a young cook who hadn't been working there all that long. "I was standing there with him one day when he went very still. He was totally taken aback. He said to me, 'Do you see that?' I told him I didn't see anything. But he said, 'Don't you see that? Don't you see that face floating there in mid-air?' I didn't see anything, but he said that's all there was, just a face. No body or anything else. He was very adamant that what he saw was a man's face."

She remembers that another day, when one of the servers was leaving the kitchen, he became transfixed on something he was seeing just over her shoulder. "He insisted that he saw a presence over my shoulder, and he also said he saw several lights hovering around whatever it was. Again, I didn't see it, but this fellow was convinced something was there."

However, one day something happened that finally convinced Donna that ghosts were, indeed, present. "On that night, I was sitting and waiting in the dining room for my daughter to come home. It was late, and I didn't want her coming in and setting off the alarms. The place was empty and dark. All of a sudden, I looked up and saw a beam of light going directly across the dining room. There was no explanation for the light. I could never find the source. It's little things like that that at the time they happen you think, well, it's nothing…but maybe it is something."

Then there was the day Donna was leaning against the upstairs bar waiting for her daughter, who, by this time, was working in the pub. "Very, very distinctly, I heard a young person's voice call for its mother. 'Mom! Mom!' the voice said. It had a very impatient tone to it. I just thought it was my daughter telling me that she was ready. I turned around to see what she wanted, but there was absolutely no one there. I have no doubt I heard the voice. When I looked in the opposite direction from where the voice had come, I saw my daughter across the kitchen talking to one of the workers. There is no way it could have been her—no way. I know I had heard voices before that day, but I always dismissed them, thinking that since we were close to the street, it was just someone outside, but this time I thought, wow, I really heard this. I really heard this voice this time, there's no doubt about that. It was very, very distinct. It was female and it was young."

After William Alexander Henry and his family left Halifax, the family of a gentleman who was the head of the Navy League, which is the building located next to Henry House, moved into the manor. Hanging in the main entrance of the restaurant is a picture of this family in a horse-drawn carriage. Apparently, Donna says, the child shown in the carriage died of whooping cough in Henry House. There is a theory that at least some of the phenomena associated with the house could be related to the death of that young girl.

Over the years, paranormal investigators have often visited Henry House hoping to find logical or scientific explanations for these occurrences. "These people have been here several times, and they agree there are things going on here that you can't explain, such as an immediate and drastic drop of temperature in the back basement storage room where Bill had his experiences with the lights. Dropping 15 degrees in a matter of seconds cannot be explained."

That storage room has been connected to other strange occurrences, Donna says. For instance, the entrance to the room is closed off with a heavy security door and latch that fasten tightly. "One day, one of our employees was making his way to the room with another employee who was behind him. The first fellow was carrying a heavy load of recyclable materials, which we store in that room. He had his hands full, and just as he was about to put the recyclables down to open the door, the door opened by itself and remained open for several minutes, as if someone was holding it. The employee placed the load of bottles inside the room, said 'thank-you' and quickly walked away. The other guy that was with him insists it happened. He said if he hadn't seen it for himself, he wouldn't have believed it. That door opened and closed by itself. Our employees are absolutely convinced of that, and there is no way it could do that, not on its own power."

While strange phenomena seem to happen throughout the entire building, Donna says the basement where the pub is located attracts the most activity. "You can always hear things that go bump down there, even when you're alone and particularly when it's late. At night, the air down there is just so heavy that it closes in on you. It's the strangest feeling. It's not a feeling of anything evil or bad, it's a feeling that something's not right down there. One of our regular customers refuses to use the lower level washrooms because she insists she sees someone pacing back and forth in the hallway. There are times at night that I can't go down there. It just feels wrong, somehow. I can't explain it, but it's like an overwhelming feeling of sadness comes over me."

Paranormal investigators agree the basement is a hotbed of activity. They have found large energy fields there, suggesting some sort of phenomena, and these energy fields usually wreak havoc on their equipment, draining their batteries and sending video equipment into a tail-spin. Some investigators insist they have recorded voices in the ambient air in the areas believed to be haunted. "Once," Donna says, "while I was telling some of the investigators about the child who died of whooping cough, they believe they recorded the word 'contagious' in the background. Another time, while I was being recorded walking down the staircase and saying that the ghosts aren't bad, they recorded what they believe is, 'thank you.' That's their interpretation, but if you listen closely, you can certainly hear something on the tape, something that shouldn't be there."

The mysteries surrounding the historic Henry House have intrigued ghost chasers and paranormal researchers for many years, to say nothing about the questions the occurrences raise for the property's owners. However, there are more questions than answers about the house, and there are few clues as to who or what may be responsible for these strange experiences. Does the ghost of William Alexander Henry, one of the Fathers of Confederation, still roam his stately Halifax manor? Does the spirit of a little girl who is believed to have succumbed to whooping cough many decades ago continue to haunt the house? Could it be that the servants who once worked in the home are still carrying out their duties, but in another time dimension? Why does so much paranormal energy seem to collect within the walls of the building, particularly in the basement? Answers to these questions may never be found.

Poison Ivy Haunts White Point

White Point Beach Resort is one of Nova Scotia's premier resort getaways located on the province's picturesque south shore. The resort's website says it best:

"We believe that this success has come to us because of the feeling that exists at White Point. It's a feeling that comes with knowing that your bartender's grandfather tended the same bar in his youth. It comes from hearing the recreation staff telling the story of Ivy, who ran the dining room in the 1920s, whose ghost is said to roam the Main Lodge. It's a feeling that comes from knowing the story of the local lads of the 1940s sneaking across the footbridge to the staff houses on summer nights to court the White Point girls."

Ivy was the first wife of Howard Elliot, one of the original owners of White Point Beach Resort. She managed the resort's food and beverage department, maintaining very high standards for dining room staff. Employees, both past and present, claim that Ivy ran a tight ship. We're told she was horrid on the best of days—therefore the name Poison Ivy.

The dining room at White Point Beach Lodge in the era during which Ivy was the manager.

Even after Ivy passed away, she was reluctant to give up control of the dining room. Today, stories of Ivy's haunting run the gamut of paranormal activity and include such happenings as spoons and ladles falling off the hooks in the kitchen. The real mystery here becomes obvious when one notices that the hooks are an "S" shape, so things have to jump off them, not fall. Many of the staff relate stories of hearing their name called during pre-meal set up, when they were alone and particularly after they had done something wrong.

Stephanie Miller, a former employee at White Point Beach Resort, recalls her experiences with Ivy. "Many times late in the evening I'd be sitting in my office—located in the corner of the dining room—and I would hear footsteps coming from the front of the dining room toward the kitchen. The door of the office was usually open, yet no one would ever appear. I always believed it was Ivy either checking to make sure I was working or wanting the office for herself. As I've said many times, even after passing she was reluctant to give up control."

Stephanie recounts another incident in which she encountered Ivy. "One evening, I went downstairs for something—I can't remember exactly what. There were so many reasons to go down there. [Once there] I saw a woman out of the corner of my eye in a flowing white pant-suit type of outfit. She was passing from the kitchen stairs through to the games room. I really didn't think much of it because I had noticed another woman wearing a similar outfit when she came to dinner earlier that evening, but when I went back upstairs, the other woman was in her seat. When I asked the staff if she'd been away from the table, I was told no, and when

I thought of it, why the heck would the woman be poking around in the basement when her husband and another couple were in the dining room having dinner?" The more she thought about what she saw, Stephanie became convinced she had seen Ivy in the basement.

Johnny, one of the groundskeepers, tells a story of him and another crew member, Billy, coming one winter day to plough the roads to the resort. It was before White Point was open year-round as it is today. As the two men came past the rose bush that used to be in the middle of the driveway at the front of the main lodge, they watched as the front door opened and closed, although they hadn't seen anyone in the vicinity. Parking the truck and getting out to investigate what they had just seen, they were alarmed to notice footprints in the snow leading to the front door. Inside, on the floor, they discovered droppings of snow as if it had fallen off someone's feet. The two men searched inside and outside the lodge, but no one could be found. As far as they knew, they were the only people on the property that cold winter day.

Current employee Bruce Clattenburg has been the night engineer at White Point Beach Resort for 10 years, and he's heard all the stories about Ivy and a few other ghosts. In fact, he has a few of his own experiences. He thinks most of the ghosts of White Point are seen in winter because it's a quiet time. "I do think they're also around in the summertime, but it's so busy around here that you just don't notice them."

Bruce believes there are three ghosts at White Point. "Or at least those are ones that I know of. One is the ghost of a young boy whose family lived in the area in the 1920s. They were the West family, and the boy would have been around the age of eight or nine when he died. The boy and some friends had a little camp on one of the islands that you can see from the shore. One day, the young fellow went out on a raft by himself and never came back. People said he drowned, but they never found his body."

A few years back, Bruce was helping another one of the resort crew members pull a boat out of the water. That's when he had his first encounter with the ghostly boy of White Point. "No matter how hard we pulled, we couldn't get the boat to come ashore. It was the weirdest thing. It wouldn't move. We'd both tug on the rope, but nothing. We couldn't budge it. All the while, we could hear laughter around us, and there was no mistaking that it was the voice of a little boy. There was no doubt what it was. Of course, we thought the rope must be hooked on something in the water, so we decided to go back into the boathouse and get a canoe to go out and get it. I'd say the boat was about 10 feet from the shore, but we never got that far. As the laughter got louder we looked out and saw a young boy sitting in the boat. He was pulling the rope in and letting the boat drift out again with the waves. He wore old-style overalls and a whitish coloured shirt. We couldn't figure how the young fellow could get out there because there weren't any other boats around or anything like that. We looked at each other. We knew something wasn't right. When we looked back, the young fellow was gone. When we went back to the rope and pulled, the boat quickly came ashore—no problem. To this day, we still don't know where the boy went or who he was, but we figured it was the West boy."

About a week after that first incident, Bruce was working down by the boathouse once again when a couple came in from a boating trip. The pair was quite worked up.

"They told us that out on one of the islands they had seen a young boy, about nine years old, and he was standing on the rocks waving. They said he was wearing overalls and they said they asked the boy if he needed a lift back to shore, but he didn't say anything to them. He just kept waving as if he didn't even see the couple. Thinking that maybe something was wrong and the boy might need help, one of the other crew members jumped in a canoe and went out to the island. When he got there, the boy was nowhere to be seen and there was no sign that he had ever been there on the island. Of course, we believe it was the island where the West kid had built his cabin."

Over the years, Bruce says he's heard other stories about the boy at White Point. "One of the more popular stories is that people report seeing a young boy looking out the windows of the boathouse who sounds an awful lot like the young boy I saw, but when they go inside, there's never anyone there. We've heard that story a lot."

Another ghost that Bruce says haunts the grounds of White Point Beach Resort is that of a former caretaker. "Many people believe the ghost of an older gentleman named Danny roams White Point. He was the caretaker here in the wintertime and the chef in the summer. He stayed in cabin 20. Today, it's unit 137. I worked with him between 1978 and 1979, and he was a great guy. I considered him a really good friend. Danny worked at White Point for a long time, and everyone said he was real good friends with Ivy. Apparently he worked for her when she lived in Halifax. He looked after the property for many years."

Bruce says that after Ivy died, many people reported seeing Danny talking to someone who was never there. "I saw it myself on many occasions. When you'd go to his cabin, it was common to see him sitting by the table having a drink and having a great conversation with someone else, only there was never anyone else around. Whenever you asked him who he was talking to, he'd say Ivy was in and they were having a talk. I left and took other jobs but eventually came back to White Point. I no sooner got back than I asked others about Danny, and they told me he had died."

Danny's cabin is the site of many paranormal experiences. "We get a lot of reports of lights going on and off, and the bed would be opened up, as if waiting for an occupant. We just figured Danny was in there playing tricks. Different people reported seeing things in that cabin that they couldn't explain."

But Danny's haunting behaviour was not confined to the cabin. "One foggy evening, I ran into a couple who had just returned from a walk on the beach. They told me about seeing a man and woman come out of the fog and then suddenly disappear. The couple insisted the man and woman had been there, then they were gone. I think the man was Danny and the woman was Ivy."

As for Ivy, Bruce says, he has heard many stories, but his own encounters with her made him a believer. "There was a time when I didn't believe in that stuff, but I certainly do now. The first one occurred around the year 2000 after a major snowstorm. We had been ploughing all day, trying to keep the roads clear. That night me and one of the other guys were salting the walkways. When I got to room 55, I noticed a woman come around the corner of the building and walk toward where I was. She was wearing only a thin black coat, even though it was February with the wind blowing off the Atlantic. It was pretty cold, I remember that. As the woman got closer, I remember saying something like, 'Awful cold to be out tonight,' and she kept on going. At first I didn't pay it much attention, but as I kept on cleaning and salting the walkways, it suddenly hit me. Even though it had been snowing, the woman didn't leave any footprints. I followed her and when I was about six feet away, she just disappeared. I remember she was a tall, thin woman with long, brownish coloured hair. I couldn't see her face, but I'm convinced it was Ivy. I couldn't tell if she was an older woman or young. Some people have seen her in her earlier years, but others have seen her as she was when she got older."

The second time Bruce encountered Ivy happened in winter 2005–06. "They called me from the front desk with a report that the heat in room 206 wasn't working, and they needed it turned on. I went to the room by way of the back stairs, which went to the upper level from the kitchen. It was the way staff travelled. On the way back down I heard the heavy security door at the top of the stairs open and close. At first I thought it was a guest, but we don't allow the guests to travel that way. Then I saw a figure. I couldn't tell if it was a man or woman, but it was moving quickly. It came by me and went into the kitchen. It was something. I could feel it as it went by, and it was cold." Bruce points out that Ivy always travelled down that stairwell to get to the kitchen.

Reports connected to Ivy have been a regular occurrence over the years. "I remember one day when I was working from 11:00 at night to 7:00 in the morning. There were two guests staying in room 212, which was Ivy's room when she was at the lodge. The guests called the front desk around

5:00 in the morning to report that their bathroom light kept coming on."

Checking out the bathroom, Bruce determined there was nothing wrong with the electricity. The switch was in good working order, he says, adding that the male guest also reported that when he went to bed, rolled over and looked into the bathroom, he could see the picture of a woman hanging where the bathroom mirror was supposed to be. "He said the woman in the picture had long hair with flowers in it. She was a nice-looking woman, he observed."

Another time, Bruce says, a guest staying in the same room came down for breakfast. She told one of the servers that she had been frightened through the night when she woke up and saw a woman standing beside her bed. She described the woman as being very thin, with flowers in her long hair. Ivy loved flowers; she wore them in her hair a lot."

Bruce says based on the stories he's heard, he understands why the ghost has earned the nickname Poison Ivy. "One night, as one of our pool guys turned out the pool lights, he had a run-in with our special guest. We're talking about sodium lights. When you shut them off and turn them back on, these lights don't come back on right away. It takes a while for them to heat up, even if they were just turned out. As the staff member turned out the lights and went to go out the door of the pool room, the lights immediately came on. There's no way they could do that even if someone else turned the switch back on. He went back in to the control panel and turned them off again. As he went to leave the room, the lights came on again. So he went back to where the switch was, and this time, the lights went out on their own. It freaked him out so he went to leave, but the door was locked. You can't lock these pool doors from the inside. He tried them all, but they were locked. He went to the light panel, turned the lights on again, and as they slowly became illuminated, the doors opened. There was no way to explain any of that."

Bruce continues. "There was the time a woman who was staying in Ivy's room woke up and saw a silhouette of a woman in the mirror. She left and never went back there. Another time, at night, two of the girls who work in the recreation department walked past the dining room on their way to the main desk to turn in their keys like they have to do every night. At one of the tables by the window overlooking the shoreline, there was a woman sitting there staring out at the waves. They knew the dining room was closed, but they thought one of the guests was sitting there enjoying the scenery. When they looked the second time, the woman was gone. They later learned that the location was Ivy's favourite table, and she would often come there and sit at night to watch the waves breaking on the shore just outside the dining room window."

Bruce says there were many reports of unusual activity over the years at the resort. "Candles kept lighting on their own and wouldn't go out. We've had reports of music playing in some rooms, even though the radios and televisions have not only been turned off, but also unplugged. Everyone who has worked at the front desk has heard footsteps going through the dining room late at night, and one morning, one of the clerks said she could hear wine glasses tinkling together even though the dining room was completely empty. It's spooky, there's no question about that."

Yes, spooky indeed.

A Haunting at Churchill Mansion Inn

Churchill Mansion is reputed to be haunted by its original owner.

Stationed high upon a hill, overlooking two emerald green lakes and the famous tidal bore of the Bay of Fundy, stands a stately old house known as the Churchill Mansion. Located on the main highway 15 kilometres from the town of Yarmouth, Nova Scotia, the house has played an important role in Maritime history for well over a century. Today, the house is a country inn that attracts guests not only from around this world, but, according to some witnesses, from the other world as well.

Robert A. Benson is the owner and manager of Churchill Mansion Inn. Bob, as he insists on being called, bought the property in 1981 with the purpose of operating it as a country inn. He talks of the home's original owner with a certain flair and a generous dose of pride, almost as if he is part of the family. "Aaron Flint Churchill," Bob proudly declares, "was a hero of the sea."

Robert A. Benson, current owner and manager of Churchill Mansion, is shown in the main entryway. Behind him is a portrait of Aaron Flint Churchill, the original owner.

Bob explains that the story begins with the ship named *Research*. On November 10, 1866, the *Research* was commanded by Captain George William Churchill of Yarmouth. Sailing with Captain Churchill on this voyage of the *Research* was his nephew, Aaron Flint Churchill, who had just turned 16. The ship sailed from Quebec with a load of lumber, bound for Scotland. After a stormy passage through the Straits of Belle Isle, the *Research* ran into a vicious northwest gale and a heavy sea struck the rudder, breaking it just below the case. Realizing their predicament, Captain Churchill rigged a jury rudder, and it was young Aaron Churchill who went over the stern, into the frigid water, to attach it. Despite the obvious danger, the boy managed to rig the jury rudder and was pulled back to the deck half-frozen.

However, the gear soon broke and still another jury rudder was made, and over the stern one more time went young Aaron—and so it went over the course of the storm. With a determination shown by Nova Scotian skippers and their crews, an eighth rudder was made, and this time it worked. The weather moderated, and the *Research* was brought to the entrance of the Firth of Clyde after a passage of 88 days from Quebec. That voyage was subsequently christened "The Voyage of Many Rudders."

Aaron Churchill spent eight more years at sea after his heroic feat. By the time he reached the age of 21, he had risen to the rank of captain. After quitting the sea at the age of 24, he went to Savannah, Georgia, where he eventually became one of the most prominent and widely known businessmen in the United States. It was while in Savannah that he invented a cotton baling press that saved the cotton industry many millions of dollars yearly.

Although he had reached the top of the ladder of success, Churchill never forgot his native Nova Scotia. He commissioned the 21-room home in Yarmouth that became a haven for him and his wife each summer. He called his house the Anchorage. Aaron Churchill passed away in Savannah on June 10, 1920. Upon his death, his remains were brought home and buried in the private family cemetery in Yarmouth.

While Churchill and his home have an undeniable place in Nova Scotian history, Churchill Mansion is also well known for another reason—it is said to be haunted. Bob is matter of fact when he explains that over the years there have been many reports of apparitions and unexplained phenomena in the country inn. "Undeniably," he says, "there is a lot of history here—and a few ghost stories as well."

Most notably, Bob explains, are the many sightings of glowing orbs encountered throughout the inn. "We believe they're energy orbs, and they've been caught hundreds of times in pictures. Many people have seen them." He describes the orbs as round circles of pulsating light that float around the rooms.

Other people, he adds, have reported seeing the figure of a woman. On many occasions, people have witnessed the apparition of a lady in white around the nearby lake and on the grounds outside the house. And at least one guest of the inn bolted down the stairs in the middle of the night claiming she had been held down by a figure and it—a man—wouldn't let her go. "We know the place is haunted," Bob says, adding that most people appear to take the strange happenings in stride.

When he purchased the property, Bob decided to retain the house in its original state. "I tried to keep as much of the original design as possible. When people come here, I want them to enjoy staying in the home as it existed more than a century ago. To me, that's what the experience of staying in Churchill Mansion is all about. It's very important to maintain that authentic atmosphere." He adds that he believes that atmosphere also contributes to the paranormal experience. Churchill Mansion offers eight guest rooms, all decorated in various motifs from a century ago, many of which still boast the original wall coverings.

Several paranormal phenomena have been reported in Aaron Churchill's niece Lottie's bedroom.

Over the years, Bob says the guests have experienced a wide range of ghostly encounters, but one of the common reports is of things that disappear and reappear in the rooms. "We think the ghosts are just playing around, but it happens fairly often. One morning a few years ago, I remember one of the guests coming down from her room and telling us she had searched her room from top to bottom but could not find her room key. She asked if we had a second key so that when she returned in the evening she would be able to get back inside. Of course we did, and when she came back that evening, we let her in the room. Once inside though, much to her surprise, she found her key neatly placed in the centre of the pillow on her bed. To this day, no one can explain how that key got there. The guest insisted she had searched the bed many times before leaving in the morning. If it had been there, surely she would have found it."

Another time, Bob says, a similar thing happened with a guest who couldn't find her sunglasses. "Normally, the woman said, she wouldn't have cared, but they were prescription sunglasses, so they were important to her. This time, I helped the woman search the room. We turned that room upside down. I even shook out all the bedding, but we couldn't find the glasses. Later in the day, after the guest had gone—without the glasses, I might add—as the staff was making up the room for the evening arrivals, one of them asked me what she should do with the glasses she had found on the bed. Now I know they weren't there in the morning. I had searched that bed myself, several times. I couldn't explain that any more than I could explain the missing room key." It is things such as this, Bob says, that lead them to believe the inn is haunted.

And there are other reports that add credence to the paranormal theory. "For some reason, when people stay in what was Aaron's room, they sleep very well, particularly the women. We've never had any complaints from guests there,"

Bob says. However, he adds, the same can't be said for room number one. That would have been Lottie's, Aaron's niece, who many believe was actually his illegitimate daughter. "People who stay in that room often report disturbances and unusual activity. One morning, a guest told us she had a miserable sleep the previous night, particularly after seeing the image of a young girl floating around the room, but only from the waist up. There were no legs."

Is Churchill Mansion haunted? Does the ghost of Lottie roam the halls of the stately home perched high upon the hill? Is Aaron Churchill still visiting his beloved mansion? What are the energy orbs that float around the rooms? The only way to know for sure is to experience the place firsthand, and Bob says he's confident that once you do, you will find the answers to these questions.

Ghosts in the Basement

It's 110 years old, overlooks the town of Lunenburg, Nova Scotia, from a promontory known as Gallows Hill and is surrounded on three sides by a cemetery. Little wonder, wrote local journalist Robert Hirtle in an article in the *Bridgewater Bulletin*, that generations of Lunenburgers, many of them fraught with superstitions garnered during their seafaring days, believe that the historic Lunenburg Academy is home to more than just mere mortals. "There are stories and there are some people who say it gives off a few vibes," laughs historian Eric Croft, operator of Lunenburg Walking Tours, who usually begins his excursions outside the school's hallowed halls and occasionally conducts late-night tours in the adjoining graveyard.

The Academy in Lunenburg, Nova Scotia, is said to have a few ghosts in its basement.

Eric says popular belief that the school may be haunted probably dates back to the building's less than auspicious beginnings, when town fathers were pondering the location to build a new structure after its predecessor burned to the ground. "When the Academy was built, there were two sites chosen as possibilities to place [the building]—over on Blockhouse Hill or on Gallows Hill," he recalls. "It was a very controversial issue."

The reason for the public outcry was the history of the latter site, which, as its name suggests, was the scene of at least three incidents of post-colonial justice carried out in the form of hangings. Along with the execution of two convicted murderers, siblings known as the Boutilier brothers, perhaps the best-remembered hanging in Lunenburg was that of Peter Mailman, which took place in the decade preceding construction of the new school. "He and his wife, Mary, went berry picking," Eric explains, recalling that time in Lunenburg's storied history. "Mary took a basket and Peter took an axe, and apparently, Mary didn't come back. Peter was hanged on Gallows Hill, and 2000 people came out to watch him hang." It was a major social event. Because he was a convicted criminal, Peter Mailman was not interred in the Christian cemetery but was buried instead in the backyard of the jailhouse.

The hangings did not stop public officials from deciding to build the new school on the site of the criminals' demise. Although fierce opposition led to a tie vote among councillors on the issue, the deadlock was broken by Mayor S. Watson Oxner, who cast the deciding ballot in favour of the Gallows Hill location. "The next election came along, and he lost," Eric points out.

Whether that defeat was an omen of things to come or not is a matter of conjecture. What we do know is that in the following years, reports of strange happenings, usually occurring in the bowels of the three-storey structure, have been commonplace. "When small kids go to the washroom in the basement, they go with a friend because every now and then, a hand comes up out of the toilet and grabs bad kids," Eric explains. "On a dark, rainy day, you can just imagine [what it's like] coming down here. It's not a very inviting place to be."

That's a story Roxie Smith, chairperson of the Lunenburg Academy Foundation and a former student of the school, has also heard many times, although she is skeptical of its validity. "I can tell you in 13 years here, I've never had any indication of that," she says with authority. "It seems to me to be a story that some little tyke made up."

Roxie recalls that when she attended the school, for some young minds such as those of the primary school students, "going through those big, dark corridors would conjure up images. I know we wouldn't go to the basement alone. We went by twos, because we were scared of whatever, I don't know," she laughs. "They may very well yet [go by twos]."

Eric says that, while he personally has never seen a ghost, he has heard a myriad of similar supernatural Lunenburg-based tales, usually told by old former fishermen of the community. Their stories, such as the ones related to the Academy, have become a part of the rich and sometimes mythical folklore of the town. "They'll tell you stories about their fishing trips and things that have happened, but they won't go into specifics," he said, "because if they do that, then it really has happened as opposed to perhaps this happened."

So, is the century-old school really haunted? "You see the Academy lit up at night, and it's got that kind of aura about it that does add to the mystery," Eric says. "But I wouldn't have a problem spending a night alone there."

Would you?

*   *   *

In the Maritimes

- If a bird hits a closed window, it means someone close to you is going to die.

- If a bird flies into your house, it means someone close to you is going to die.

- If a window slams shut on its own, it means someone is going to die.

Ghosts in the Town Hall

There have been many reports of ghosts haunting Fredericton's City Hall.

When researching ghost stories, we authors often find ourselves turning to other writers for assistance. One such Maritime researcher is New Brunswick folklorist David Goss.

He has spent years chasing ghosts and writing about his exploits in various newspaper columns and books. David has graciously agreed to share this story that was originally published in the *Moncton Times & Transcript* and revised in April 2006. He writes that a century ago, there were reports of ghosts that haunted Fredericton City Hall, and today, some people claim they still lurk about.

This is what the *Fredericton Daily Gleaner* had to say about the matter on January 30, 1896:

"The City Hall Ghost.

"It Continues to Make Things Lively for Everybody.

"A couple of young men who were about the City Hall Tuesday night tell of a genuine ghost they saw flitting through the corridors and about the council chamber. It appears they were on their way to the dressing rooms via the council chamber, when an object dressed in white with a strip of black about its neck, a dark covering over its feet and white whiskers blocked their progress just outside of the council chamber. Then they say it scooted across toward Col. Marsh's office and disappeared.

"The young men continued on their way through the council chamber, and when in the middle of the room the ghost appeared before them again for an instant only. Then it shot across the room like a flash and was gone. One of the youths fell back in a faint in the arms of his companion, who was in a poor state to support even a feather just then, shaking and shivering as he was. Since Mr. Burchill heard the mysterious knockings lately, some queer sounds are reported by officials, but the ghost seems only to make its appearance to strangers and reveal its presence to officials by poundings only. Those who are in the habit of spending a night now and then in the lock-up should strive to break it off, as that City Hall ghost is death on intruders, and liable to make it hot for some of them one of these nights."

David says the references here are to the second-level city council chambers still in use, and to the ground-level City Hall lock-up, which is no longer used to house prisoners but is still a part of the building. "As part of a series of stories I did on New Brunswick ghosts, I asked tourism officer and long-time worker at Fredericton City Hall, Nancy Lockerbie, to pass the story as printed above among some of the current staff in City Hall who had a long association with the building and who work late into the night on various projects to see what sort of comments she received."

Linda Dykeman said, "I've never really seen anything but always had a strange feeling there was a presence in the building when I was alone or working late with someone else. I tried never to work alone because of this feeling…"

"In my first year at City Hall [1997]," Wendy Bradley noted, "I thought I saw something in the council chamber. I went upstairs to turn out the lights, and on my way out, I turned around and thought I saw something in front on Prince Frederick's painting." Next day in the kitchen, Wendy reported hearing banging coming from upstairs, where the council chamber is located. She said she would not go up there alone for the next couple of years, though she has no problem doing so now. She said, "During that year, I think a lot of us had some experiences. It was the consensus that something was lurking around."

Alex Forbes does not believe there is anything to the story. "I have been through every inch of the building, particularly at night, and haven't seen a thing." However, the tale did remind him that he was previously asked to comment on such a sighting by a former employee, Jim Woodford, who claimed to have seen a ghost in their office, which is located where the old jail or lock-up had been in 1896. "It seemed to freak him out, whatever it was," Alex said, adding, "I guess ghosts only show themselves to certain people."

Alex's position is also held by Bruce Noble, who stated candidly that, being a descendant of one of the witches hanged in 1692 in Salem, he should have the inside track to knowledge of a ghost in the building, but noted, "I simply have never heard or seen such apparitions."

So, opinions seem evenly divided between those who believe and those who do not believe in the ghosts of Fredericton City Hall. There's only one thing left to do, and tourism officials in Fredericton would be delighted if you made a visit to the capital city of New Brunswick to check out for yourself if the building still has ghosts lurking about.

Yarmouth's Haunted Jail

Yarmouth, a major fishing and ferry port located on the Gulf of Maine in southwestern Nova Scotia, is sometimes referred to as "The Gateway to Nova Scotia." Initially called Port Forchu, Yarmouth was laid out in 1759 and incorporated in 1890. Throughout the 19th century, the town was a major shipbuilding centre, but when steamships started to take over, the town declined in status. Tourism has been a major industry in Yarmouth since the late 19th century.

Within the town boundaries is one of Nova Scotia's oldest jails and, not surprisingly, it is said to be haunted. The Yarmouth County Jail, built in 1864, functioned as a place of incarceration for local criminals until 2004, when it was shut down by the provincial government. Although the jail is still standing today, it remains vacant.

Yarmouth County Jail, built in 1864, has a few ghosts roaming its corridors.

The most famous trial held at the courthouse took place in 1922 when the Supreme Court tried Omar P. Roberts for the murder of his housekeeper, Flora Gray. Roberts was subsequently convicted and became the last person to be hanged in Yarmouth County. But did he really leave the jail upon his death?

Over the years, many witnesses have reported strange phenomena at the Yarmouth County Jail. Supposedly, three ghosts haunt the structure. One ghost is said to be that of a man who, many years ago, is believed to have been burned alive in one of the jail cells. Documentation to support this story is in short supply, but local legend says it is so. Over the years, there have been reports of hearing a man crying out in pain and of smelling a pungent, disgusting odour, such as one would expect from burning flesh. Who the man was and why or how he was burned remains a mystery.

The second ghost said to roam the corridors of the old jail house is that of a woman. Again, information about the woman's origin or why she haunts the old jail is in short supply, but right up until the facility closed, many people reported having seen a woman roaming the hallways, and others said they clearly heard the unmistakable high-heeled footsteps of a woman walking the halls, particularly in the visitors' area. Upon investigation, however, no one was ever found to be there.

The third ghost said to inhabit the former jail is that of Omar P. Roberts. It is easy to assume that the tragic circumstances surrounding his death explain his presence in the old structure. Over the years, many witnesses reported seeing a man roaming about, but upon a second look, it seemed the man was never really there after all. Other witnesses at the jail reported a variety of strange phenomena such as things moving about, strange pounding noises that defied logical explanation and sudden and drastic temperature changes.

When the government of Nova Scotia closed the jail, security guards were posted at the building to ward off vandals or other intruders until it could be locked up. One of the guards stationed there was Don Roberts, who worked the midnight shift for about seven weeks in spring 2004. Being alone in such a building in the middle of the night can be an unnerving arrangement, Don agrees, but it is particularly so in a place said to be haunted. "I had heard all the stories about the ghosts," he said, "but I wasn't taken to believe in such things—most of the time. But some of the guys were spooked by the place. We had this one guy working for us who refused to work the night shift. There was just no way he was going to be there overnight all by himself."

Don had no problem working the night shift, and he did so for several weeks without incident until one night. "It was just the strangest thing," Don says, insisting without hesitation that he is 100 percent certain that he was alone in the building that night. "There is absolutely no doubt that no one else was there."

For the first few hours of the shift, everything went along as normal. However, around 3:30 AM, he heard the sound of running water. The only sinks in the facility are at the end of each corridor in the bathrooms, and Don could tell that's where the sound was coming from. "Now keep in mind, there was no one else in the building, so I thought I better go investigate to see where that running water was coming from. It was time to do my rounds anyway. But as soon as I got up from my chair, the water stopped running. Just like that, it stopped. Now I thought that was pretty strange, so I sat back down again and, no kidding here, just as soon as I did, I heard the water start running again. It spooked me, that's for sure, because I could hear it. I thought, well, okay, this is too much, so I better go investigate. When I got up the second time, the water stopped again."

Don slowly made his way down the corridor to the small bathroom. "When I got there, I found the water taps were turned off tight. But when I felt the sinks, they were wet. There's just no way taps can turn on and off by themselves."

And since there was no one else in the building that night, Don can't explain how the water could be turned on and off. "It's just a weird thing," he says. "That happened to me twice in that building and it spooked me both times. I put it in my report and thought nothing else of it."

On a different occasion, again while Don was working the night shift, he had a second brush with the paranormal. Again he was alone. Like before, for the first part of the shift, everything was quiet. He was suddenly startled when something hit him in the back of the head. "All of a sudden without warning, this bulletin board that had been hanging on the wall in the office for years just came down and hit me on the head," Don says. "I don't know how it came off the wall. But it did, and it startled me pretty good, I'll admit that."

Don remained on the job for a few more weeks until the contract was complete, but he says even to this day he cannot explain how those things could have happened. However, after relating these incidents to others in the town, Don learned about the tragic story of Omar Roberts and discovered that he is a distant relative of the convicted murderer who was hanged in the old jail house. "That is a bit unsettling," he admits.

Was the ghost of Omar Roberts reaching out and trying to make contact with a long-lost relative? Or were the other ghosts in the jail trying to chase off the intruders? Who can say for sure, but those who have witnessed the hauntings firsthand insist that something out of the ordinary happens in that building—something that defies explanation.

*　　*　　*

In the Maritimes

- If you hear three knocks at your door, but there is no one there, that's called a token and it means someone in your family is going to die.

- If you see the vision of someone who isn't really there, that's called a forerunner and it's a sign of imminent death for someone close to you.

Saint John Haunts

Make no mistake about it, Valerie Evans of Saint John, New Brunswick, is a believer in ghosts. New Brunswick researcher and author David Goss says Valerie has brought her eerie tales to life in her popular "Murder Mystery" presentations that she does with her husband, Alistair, all over the province. She's had them appear on the uptown streets as part of "Character Walks." They've come slipping out of the mists clinging to Lily Lake in Rockwood Park, and she regularly shows where they are believed to dwell on tours of the city she conducts by coach and on foot. She says, "I'm not trying to convince anyone that this city is overrun with ghosts, but people love meeting these folks from the past, and so when we say we're having a ghost walk, you can be sure you will get people's attention."

According to David, Valerie has had her own run-ins with ghosts and knows firsthand the tingle of excitement that ghosts and ghost stories always create. "I guess it sort of gets the adrenaline flowing," she says. "It's like going on a roller-coaster ride—you feel a little threatened, it's a bit dangerous, a little scary. People just like the thrill, the excitement. With ghost stories, there is always the possibility that what you're telling them just could be true."

Valerie's own experiences include living in an old house on Mecklenburg Street in the city's south end, where she became convinced ghosts were real enough. "When I do tours, I always show off the house near the old Board of Health building that I lived in many years ago. There was a basement door that I was worried about, so one time

I asked a fellow tenant, Barry King, to fasten it solidly because he was going out of town. When I went down after he'd left, the door was wide open again. I thought, 'Well, he must have forgotten to fasten it,' so I proceeded to close it and hook it. It just flew open again. So I tried again, and again, and each time it just flew open, so I pulled on it really hard, fastened it and held it. The door literally shook in my hands until it flung open once again so violently that I had to jump out of the way. I said, 'Well, whatever wants this door to be open is pretty determined, and if it wants it open it can stay open as far as I am concerned.' And it did."

It was after that incident that Valerie started offering tours, and along with historical tidbits, she occasionally tells of ghosts known to be present in some of the homes and businesses she is pointing out. "People really love to hear such stories and often add to what I know," Valerie says. Today, she has a half-dozen stories she uses regularly—and a few that she can't use any longer because the buildings have been torn down.

Among the latter is one about a student nurse known only as Margaret. She worked at the old General Hospital that stood on Waterloo Street. Margaret once improperly propped a baby's bottle in its mouth. The child choked and died, and Margaret, distraught at her deed, committed suicide by jumping off the rooftop. After that, late at night, she would be seen as a shadow in the backlit windows carrying the child she neglected. Hospital staff would feel Margaret's presence in the nursery in the form of a cold aura which would sweep through the room, and soon after, an empty rocking chair would begin to move.

When the Lancaster Veterans Hospital was still standing on Prince Street (West), Valerie would tell of a room that was part of the old Jewett Mansion, around which the hospital had been built, that was thought to have a ghost of one of the Jewett family occupying it. If the door to the room was shut, it would fling open; if left open, it would close. Patients in the room were never comfortable, so eventually the hospital staff walled it over and let it be.

Where the ghosts go when buildings are torn down is a mystery to Valerie. She has never heard of any of them moving to other places. But she does know of many other Saint John ghosts she can point out. One of her favourites is the story of the ghost of Senator McLean in the old CFBC building on Carleton Street. McLean was the owner of Connors Brothers and was known to hand out sardines to the staff at Christmas. Staff in the building knew his ghost was present if they caught the strong odour of sardines. Valerie adds, "Tom Young once told me that McLean's ghost was quite a trickster. When there was only one guy on duty late at night, he'd leave the control booth and go out to the washroom, and come back to find all the lights out. Some staff got so spooked, they never came back to work."

At what became the Parker House Inn, Valerie says, "The ghost of Mrs. White, for whom the house was built as a wedding gift, still shows up to check her home, and they know she's around when she sets the spinning wheel into motion."

Just a few blocks south, at a popular bed and breakfast called Mahogany Manor, she adds, "The spirit of the wife of the first minister of adjacent Germain Street Baptist Church is said to come walking down the stairs holding an old lantern."

Ghosts at the Halifax Citadel

When the British founded Halifax in 1749, they were attracted to its tremendous harbour and the high hill overlooking the harbour and its approaches. On this hill, the British constructed the central fortress for the defence of the new town and naval base. They named it the Citadel.

The fortress has been rebuilt several times over the past two and a half centuries. The top of the hill itself has been lowered an estimated 12 to 20 metres through all the construction and levelling. The first fortification of any real permanence on the hill began in 1761. The present Citadel, completed in 1856, is the fourth in a series of forts since 1749 to occupy the hill overlooking the harbour. It is an excellent example of a 19th-century bastion fortification complete with defensive ditch, ramparts, musketry gallery, powder magazine and signal masts. Although never attacked, the fort was garrisoned by the British Army until 1906 and by Canadian Forces during World War I and World War II.

The fourth Citadel was established to guard against a land-based attack from the United States. The massive, star-shaped masonry fortification took 28 years to build. Constructed originally as a smoothbore fortification, the Halifax Citadel quickly became obsolete with the introduction of powerful rifle guns in the 1860s. In response to the rapidly changing times, the Halifax Citadel upgraded its armaments and, for the first time, could defend the harbour as well as the land approach because the new artillery fired heavier shells a greater distance and with more accuracy.

The major role for the Halifax Citadel after 1900 was to provide barrack accommodations and act as a command centre for other harbour defences. When World War II broke out in 1939, the Halifax Citadel was used as a temporary barracks for troops going overseas and as the centre for anti-aircraft operations for Halifax. The Halifax Citadel was the "last view of the country for many thousands outward bound and the first landmark to those who returned."

Today, the Halifax Citadel is operated by Parks Canada and is recognized as one of the most important historic sites in Canada. It has been restored to the mid-Victorian period with a living history program featuring the 78th Highland Regiment, the Royal Artillery, soldiers' wives and civilian tradespersons. Guided tours, an audiovisual presentation and modern exhibits communicate its historical themes. Beyond its historical importance, though, some people claim the fortress is haunted by the ghosts of soldiers and early settlers who hoped to create a new life in Halifax.

Hal Thompson is an administrative officer with the Halifax Regimental Association, a nonprofit group contracted by Parks Canada to do service work at the Citadel. He started there as a summer employee in 1987. The self-proclaimed history nut describes himself as an amateur researcher and writer. "This is a great place to work for someone like me," he says. "There's so much history here that you never run out of material. There's lots of inspiration here."

Hal became interested in the Citadel's ghosts after hearing countless stories from colleagues and visitors who claimed to have witnessed unexplained phenomena at the site. "There are so many people who say they've seen things or heard things that I finally decided that someone had to write them down." The result is a self-published book called *Ghosts of the Halifax Citadel*.

According to eyewitnesses, ghosts have been seen throughout the Citadel for decades, and one of the most common places of reported spiritual activity is at a location known as the Tides of History. Built in the mid-1970s, the structure houses historical exhibits and four mini theatres where audiovisual presentations relating the story of the founding of Halifax and the history of the Citadel are shown daily at regular intervals. Each theatre presents a 15-minute short film, so visitors can spend a good hour at the location. For security reasons, each theatre contains closed-circuit television cameras, and that is where the ghosts come in.

"The equipment is getting a little dated now, but it still works fine and it does what it's supposed to do," Hal begins. "The Tides of History is a mysterious place, there's no question about that. People have often said they hate to be in the place alone, especially after hours. And at least one maintenance staff member claims, although she was alone at the time, she has heard her name spoken into her ear on two separate occasions while cleaning in there, but the events took place several years apart."

Stories such as these cause Hal to wonder if, indeed, ghosts do inhabit the Citadel. "Beyond that incident," he continues, "we've had lots of reports of strange sounds, of doors opening and closing on their own and of hearing footsteps when there is no one around."

Hal says while all of this was interesting, "It wasn't earth-shattering and, until I was present when one of these events happened, I wasn't sure if I believed all this stuff." Today, he admits, it's a different story. "After seeing it for myself, I know something spiritual is connected with that place."

Theatre number four is the most common location for these hauntings. "Many strange things happen there. For instance, we've had reports from staff of seeing someone in the theatre's display area on the closed circuit monitor at a time when the theatres were closed. Obviously thinking a visitor may have gotten in there by accident, the staff member goes to the theatre to help them out, but when they get there, the theatre is empty. There is just no way anyone could have gotten by a staff member on their way out without being seen. That just can't happen. I didn't believe this occurred until I saw it for myself."

Hal remembers a day when a staff member was sitting at the desk in the monitoring room glancing at the closed-circuit screens and reading a book. It was April or May, just before the busy tourist season was to begin, and it was very quiet at the Citadel with everything running smoothly until the staff member looked up at the monitor for theatre number four. She saw what she later described as an outline of a head and shoulders directly in front of the camera. "I was there. I saw it," says Hal. "It was more than a little unnerving. We went directly to theatre four to see who was in there, but the place was empty. Now, considering the camera is mounted at least 10 feet off the floor, there is no way anyone could have been standing that close to it. We tried to duplicate what we had seen on the monitor, but there is no way anyone could get their body into that position. We still can't explain what we saw on the monitor." Some things defy explanation, he agrees.

Hal says he knows of at least two other staff members who have reported similar experiences. "One young woman says she saw a man in a dark suit standing in the World War

Ghostly images have been seen on this bank of monitors by employees at the Halifax Citadel.

II display in there. He was going through some papers that were on an old desk from that era. She jumped up and ran to the theatre. There was no one there, and she says the papers had not been touched or moved. And in theatre three, another employee claims to have seen on the monitors a dark figure roaming about, but upon investigation could not find anyone there."

Hal says it may be hard to believe these events can happen, but after witnessing them himself, he is now convinced that something is going on there. "I mean, there is just no explanation for these encounters. For example, you have to manually turn off the cameras in the theatres with the switch on the camera. We've had many reports of the camera in theatre four being turned off even when we know no one has been in there. How do you explain things like that?"

Hal points out that the unusual phenomena are not limited to the theatres. Ghostly images and voices have been reported at various locations throughout the fortress, including the old Victorian-era schoolhouse and the barracks buildings, but especially the prison holding cells, where hundreds of people were kept at various times in the Citadel's history. At one point in the 1840s, they had up to 40 people crammed into those little cells at a time. "We don't know why," he says. "But this is a dark, dingy place, and it surely would not have been very comfortable for those people."

Access to the prison cells can only be gained from the ramparts in the fortress wall and by descending 33 steps. "It's not a very nice place, and back then they would have used these locations to defend the fort. When you're down there, you can feel the depression. The place just closes in on you, and it's very common to hear many strange noises and footsteps when there is no one there. I guess that's only natural for a place like this."

Considering the long and storied history of the Halifax Citadel, Hal adds, it's only natural that ghosts would be seen there. Natural, indeed.

2
Haunted Houses

more than 150 years, the house, local residents claim, contains the souls of some previous occupants. While the current tenants do not wish to reveal their identity or disclose the exact location of their property for fear of an invasion of their privacy, they are willing to tell of their encounters with the supernatural. For our purposes then, we shall refer to the homeowners as Bob and Diane. Their story begins some 20 years ago when they moved into the house on a quiet, tree-lined street in this quaint town located in the heart of New Brunswick's dairy country.

The couple admit that before purchasing the stately two-storey manor, they had heard stories about ghosts that supposedly haunted the place, roaming freely from room to room as if they still existed in this world and in this time. However, Bob and Diane were not believers. They quickly dismissed the stories as local superstition or the work of overactive imaginations. "We just didn't buy it," says Bob, his voice trailing off as if hesitant to express his next thought.

"But things are different today," Diane pipes up, finishing her husband's thought. "Now, we'll swear on a stack of bibles that the place is haunted. We've seen too many things to think otherwise. Even Bob believes, and if you can convince him, then you know something's going on."

"There's not much doubt," Bob reluctantly continues, almost afraid to reveal the secrets hidden within the walls of his historic house. Finally, he says, "We have ghosts, and you can believe that."

Both Bob and Diane admit that when they first purchased their home, they were skeptical that such things existed, but after living there for more than two decades, they are now convinced that ghosts reside with them. For about the first year that they lived in their home, everything appeared normal, and the couple believed that all the stories they had heard about ghosts before moving in had been nothing more than local folklore. They were about to learn that they were wrong—dead wrong.

Diane says it was about three weeks short of their first anniversary in the house when she first encountered the ghost. Early one morning while she was getting ready for work in the upstairs bathroom, she was startled by a quick drop in the room temperature. "All of sudden," she explains, "it got very, very cold in there. In fact, it got so cold that I could practically see my breath, and it was the middle of July, so even though this is old house is drafty, there's no way it was that cold in there."

She admits that the immediate temperature drop sent shivers up her spine for more reasons than one. "I was spooked. It just didn't feel right. I can't explain it, but it just felt odd and I suddenly felt very, very sad, like I had just received some bad news or something."

Quickly finishing at the sink so she could get out of the room, Diane happened to glance in the mirror and was frightened to see a white mist floating near the doorway. "It was only there for a second and then it was gone. I only got a quick glimpse of it the mirror, but I know it was there. There was no shape or form to it. It was just sort of like a cloud, there one second, gone the next. I don't how else to explain it."

Bob jumps in, "Whatever it was, I know it scared the bejesus out of her." Already down in the kitchen on the ground floor preparing to make breakfast, Bob says he heard a scream from the bathroom that sounded like someone had, well, just seen a ghost. "I really thought something bad had happened to Diane. I don't think I've ever heard her scream like that."

Running up the stairs as quickly as his legs could carry him, Bob found Diane in the bathroom shivering. "I mean, she was shaking from head to toe. She was terrified. I knew something had to have happened for her to be that frightened. When she was finally able to tell me what had happened, I didn't know what to say, but I knew whatever it was, it sure left an impact on her."

After that morning, unusual things began happening on a more regular basis. "It's a variety of things," Bob explains. "We can lay in bed at night and hear someone come up the full flight of stairs from the kitchen to the hallway, then the footsteps stop as if someone has paused at the top landing to look around. After a few seconds, the footsteps start again, and they always come in the direction of our bedroom. But they usually stop just outside the door. We never see anything. We just hear the footsteps three, sometimes, four or five times a month."

But that isn't all. The couple shares their home with three cats: Nicky, Amber and Skippy. They say watching their pets' behaviour can sometimes tip them off that a ghost is in the room. "They just act different," Diane says. "Normally, they're very docile, loving cats, very mild mannered, but when they get spooked, their personalities change. It's like they become agitated by something in the room, and a lot of times they'll just hightail it out of there and hide. Sometimes, we don't see them for hours."

There are times, Diane says, that the cats will not go up the stairs. "They'll go to the bottom of the steps, but they won't go any farther. They stand at the bottom and hiss, and their hair will stand up on their backs. It's like they can see something. We go and look, but we can never see anything."

One of her cats, Nicky, likes to sleep on the arm of the large, overstuffed easy chair that sits in the living room where Bob watches television and where he usually falls asleep. Diane recalls one incident where Nicky, who had been curled up in a ball for most of the morning, "just fell off the arm for no obvious reason. It was like something pushed her, and it scared the poor cat half to death. This cat was used to sleeping on that arm. There's no way she lost her balance and fell off. I just can't buy that. But whatever happened, I can tell you that poor cat was out of that room quicker than you can say the word 'ghost.' She didn't come back into the living room until the next day, so I know something had to spook her really badly."

Beyond all these strange goings-on, both Bob and Diane sometimes detect unusual smells in their house. In the living room area, for example, they sometimes smell a lady's perfume. "It's very pretty," Diane says. "It's the kind of smell you would normally associate with a grandmother—very fragrant, like violets, and it lasts for a while. We smell that quite often." In the kitchen, they sometimes detect the distinct odour of a man's pipe or perhaps cigar smoke. "Sometimes it's very strong, other times it's very faint, but you know it's there." The upstairs rooms sometimes have a musty or rotting odour. "It's the kind of smell you get when burlap gets wet. It's not nice at all. In fact, it kind of burns your nose," Diane explains. "The first time we smelled that, we spent an entire day trying to find the source because we didn't want it coming back. But it comes back every now and then. Not a lot, but every now and then."

In the past 20 years, Diane and Bob say it's difficult to know how many times they've encountered the ghosts in their home. Occasionally, they say, different things will happen several times a day, while other times they can go for weeks without having an experience. And, they point out, not all their encounters are major events. Sometimes, the experience can be subtle.

For instance, Bob says, there are times when the doors on some of the rooms will not remain closed. "You might not think much of it, but you can close them and they won't stay closed." He says this is especially true with the upstairs rooms. In fact, he got so tired of trying to keep the door to one bedroom closed that he finally removed it altogether, and it remains off to this day. "The darned thing just would not stay shut. I even put a new doorknob and latch on it, but it wouldn't stay closed so I fixed it once and for all. I took if off, and as far as I'm concerned, it's staying off."

And, Diane says, it's not only the room doors that won't stay closed. "It doesn't seem to happen as often as with the rooms, but the doors on the kitchen cupboards sometimes won't stay closed. There are days when I've come down to the kitchen in the morning and found all the cupboard doors wide open. It was kind of like someone had been going through the cupboards looking for something and didn't close the doors behind themselves."

But of all the unusual occurrences in the house, it is the immediate drop of temperature they sometimes experience in the upstairs bathroom that causes them the most concern. Over the past two decades, they say it's happened seven or eight times, and Bob has experienced it only once. The other times, Diane has been in the room when it's happened. "I guess I'm the lucky one…maybe not. Of everything that happens in this house, that's the one thing that really bothers me," Diane says. "I really feel frightened when that happens because it just feels so sinister and it upsets me. It usually gives me the kind of feeling you experience when you go to a funeral parlor. I know that sounds weird, but that's how I feel. I'm empty and drained, like I've had a major upset, the kind of upset you get when you've lost a close friend or family member. I don't like it at all."

Although Bob has only once experienced the cold, he agrees with his wife. "It's the worst thing that happens in this house. She's right about that. The time it happened to me, I couldn't get it out of my mind for days. It was late in the evening, and I was in the bathroom getting ready for bed when it got really cold. It wasn't a gradual drop in temperature—it was sudden and drastic. I could actually see my breath. It lasted only two or three minutes, but it was long enough, and it sure left its mark on me."

As for the white cloud that Diane saw the first time she experienced the cold temperature, Bob has never seen that, but Diane has experienced it one other time. "It was the fourth time I had experienced the cold and, like the first time, it was there in the doorway and then it was gone. It happens very fast and you only catch a glimpse of it, but I swear it was there. For some reason this particular ghost—or whatever it is—is connected to the bathroom, and we don't why."

Bob says they do know that when the house was first built, the bathroom was originally a bedroom and the bathroom was added around the early 1900s, so it's possible that whatever this entity is, it could be connected to that. "Obviously, we just don't know."

Despite all these occurrences, even the drastic temperature drops in the bathroom, both Diane and Bob say they don't feel threatened by whatever inhabits their home. "After all this time, we don't think it, or they, means us any harm. If something was going to happen, I'm sure it would have happened long before now," Bob reasons.

Diane agrees, although she adds, "I can live with most of what happens, but I could do without the temperature drops."

*   *   *

In the Maritimes

- If a rocking chair rocks on its own, it's a sign of bad luck.

- Whistling or singing at the dinner table is bad luck.

The Ghost of the Lost Orphan

Ever heard voices and can't explain where they came from? Ever thought you'd seen something out of the corner of your eye, yet you know there is no one else with you? Ever feel like someone is watching you, yet you know you are alone? Ever think you've seen a ghost? Well, Nancy Oulton, a Maritime wife and mother of two children, has experienced all that, and she believes that there are things that happen in this world that defy any logical explanation.

Nancy lives in the rural community of Port Elgin, a fishing village in southeastern New Brunswick with a population of roughly 430. "This place is so small that we not only know our neighbours, we also know their pets' names," she jokes, but her tone quickly changes as she concedes her story is no laughing matter.

Thinking back, Nancy says her encounters with the paranormal began shortly after she and her husband moved into their home about a year after they we were married. "Unlike other stories about haunted houses I had heard over the years, our house wasn't old or anything like that. We built it ourselves, and as far as we knew, nothing unusual had ever happened on the property before we built there. Actually, the property had been the location of an apple orchard for many years, so it's unlikely it was connected to the events that happened in the house. We cleared the land ourselves and we built the house, and shortly after our first anniversary, our first child was born."

Nancy says although the events are very vivid in her memory, she isn't exactly sure at what point she started hearing the little voice. "But I know it wasn't long after the first baby was born that I started hearing the voices," she recalls. "It would wake me up at all times of the night. It could be when I was first dozing off to sleep at night, it could be in the middle of the night when everyone else in the house was fast asleep, or it could be early in the morning just before the alarm would go off. There was no rhyme nor reason to it, but I would wake up hearing this little voice holler, 'Mommy, Mommy!'"

Of course, she says, in later years she would always think the voice was that of one of her children, and she would lay awake waiting for them to call again so she would know which one of her children needed her. "Sometimes it was so real to me that I would get out of bed and go check on the kids to see if they were all right. When I got to their rooms, I usually found that they were still snug in their beds, fast asleep."

Nancy says while the voice started shortly after her first child was born, it continued for years and actually intensified upon the birth of her second baby. "I would get really worked up when my children were small, especially when they got old enough to refer to me as mommy because when I heard the other voice, I couldn't normally tell if it was a boy or girl, and that was really confusing for me. I couldn't tell if one of my own children needed me or not. Young children can be difficult to differentiate, especially when you're just waking up or just falling asleep."

The weird thing about the voice, Nancy says, was that other than herself, no one else in the house seemed to hear it. "I remember that on occasion, just as I was falling asleep, I would say to my husband, 'Did you hear that? Is there something wrong with one of the children?' and he'd be like, 'What are you talking about? I didn't hear anything.' You can imagine that would be pretty unnerving for me."

The voice continued for years, and over time Nancy tried to put it out of her mind. "I tried not to put a whole lot of thought into it. I tried not to analyze it or anything like that because it would have driven me nuts. But I just kept hearing this little child's voice calling, 'Mommy, Mommy,' and I just kept wondering where it was coming from. I found myself checking on my kids more often because I just had to reassure myself that it was not them calling for me. If I did go check on the kids, of course I'd find that they were still tucked in sound asleep, just as I had left them when they went to bed. And it never seemed as though they were having any bad dreams or anything like that, so I was always reassured that it wasn't my children I was hearing, but then it bothered me that if they weren't calling me, then who was?"

But there was still nothing to explain where the child's voice was coming from. And slowly, over the years, the voice escalated to other experiences. "After a number of years of hearing the tiny voice, I did, I guess, at times feel that there was a presence in the house with us. Sometimes, while I was sitting in the living room and looking down the hallway in the direction of the bedrooms, I would see a shadow out of the corner of my eye or I would feel the presence of someone watching me. When this started to happen, I was getting a little nervous because I was convinced that something was going on that I couldn't explain."

Then the experiences went to the next level. "It happened one night when I was getting ready to go to bed," she says. "As I do every night, I was having a glass of milk. I was standing in the kitchen without any of the kitchen lights on. The lamps from the living room gave off enough light that you could see in the kitchen. It was a simple thing. I removed the milk, left the fridge door open and went to the cupboard to pour the milk. That's when something caught the corner of my eye. When I looked back, there was a child standing beside the fridge. I just jumped. It scared the heck out of me. I just freaked out because it wasn't either of my children."

Nancy says the memory of the child she encountered in her kitchen that night is just as vivid today as it was all those years ago. "The child had short hair, but it was curly from what I could see. The child was wearing a woolen cap, and it was pulled down over its head so most of its hair was covered. But I can tell you that he or she had on a long-sleeved white blouse or shirt and a pair of pants that came to the knees. It certainly wasn't any type of clothing that my children would have worn. I blinked, and when I looked again, the child was gone. There was nothing beside the fridge. I went to bed after that, but I can tell you I didn't sleep well at all that night. I knew what I had seen, but I kept thinking that I must be going crazy. When I think back to that night, I would say the child was around eight or nine, but I couldn't tell if it was a boy or a girl."

After that incident, it was several more years before Nancy saw the child again. "But I kept hearing the voice, just the same. 'Mommy! Mommy!' it would say, often in a weak, sometimes pitiful tone." The voice would come in cycles, she says. "Sometimes it would be there almost every night; sometimes it would be weeks before I'd hear it again, but then it would come steady for a while. I never knew when I was going to hear it or when it would stop."

A few years after encountering the image of the child in her kitchen, Nancy suddenly awoke one night from a peaceful sleep. It was late, she recalls, and the moon was so bright that it illuminated the entire bedroom. "I could see around the whole room even though there were no lights on. And I swear to you that's when I saw it again. When I opened my eyes, that same child was standing at the foot my bed. It was dressed exactly the same as the other time in the kitchen. Then the child said to me, 'Help me, I'm sick. I have a fever. Please help me, help me.' It was begging and pleading with me to help. I was terrified. I thought I was dreaming, but I knew I wasn't. I didn't know what to do as I watched the child move along the foot of my bed and then go out the bedroom door. I can't remember if the door was open or closed, but regardless, it went out that way."

The experience left Nancy shaken. "I wasn't sure what I had just seen, and just coming awake like that, I wasn't sure if it was one of my children or not. I got up and went straight to check on my children. They were fine. I could tell they hadn't been out of bed, but that still didn't explain what had just happened."

After that night, Nancy was beside herself. She often heard the voice, but she was alarmed by the latest vision and by its message. She felt she needed to find help, but she didn't know where to look. Her husband didn't believe her, and she was too uncomfortable to tell anyone else. Then, one day at work, she found a sympathetic ear and some unexpected assistance.

"I used to work with a woman whose sister-in-law was said to have a gift," Nancy explains. "This one day at work, we were sharing ghost stories and just chatting about unusual things when I decided to tell her about my experiences at the house. She thought it was awesome, and she thought her sister-in-law could help me even though she lived in Ontario. My co-worker sent her sister-in-law an email telling her everything about my experiences. A few days later, the woman from Ontario contacted me and told me she felt she could help."

The Ontario woman told Nancy that she felt the spirit was that of a little girl. She said she could sense the child in the house and she believed the girl's mother had left her at an orphanage many, many years ago. The mother had told the child she would be back to get her, but she never returned, leaving the child at the orphanage for several years. The mother had dressed the girl in boys' clothing because it was felt in those days boys were easier to adopt, but the little girl got sick with a bad fever and eventually died. She felt there was a relationship between this orphanage and Nancy's house, that if the orphanage had not been located on their property, then someone had brought the spirit with them.

She told Nancy she would keep hearing and seeing and feeling this spirit until the child found her mother. "She told me she was certain the spirt was of this child who had passed away and was trying to find to find her mother," Nancy says. "She also told me that when I felt this spirit or heard it or saw it, I should tell the little girl that it was okay to visit her house, but that she should move to the light. I should tell her that her mommy was waiting for her there on the other side."

Although Nancy says she had experienced some strange things over the years, the information she received from this Ontario woman was hard to accept. "I just thought, well okay, this is really getting out of hand here, but I listened to what this woman had to say. After all, I knew better than to say these things cannot happen. Look at what had been happening to me all those years."

Some time after she received the information from the Ontario woman, Nancy had her final encounter with the child. "It had been a while since I had heard the voice, but on this particular morning while I was laying in bed, I heard it again. There wasn't anything out of the ordinary going on that morning, but from out of nowhere I began to hear the voice. It said, 'Mommy. Mommy!' This time, it became very persistent and kept getting louder. Suddenly, I heard the bedroom door open, and I heard the voice again. It said, 'Mommy! Mommy!' It was very loud and very angry. I had never heard it speak like that in the past. The tone was definitely different from previous times."

Nancy was terrified. She wondered if she had somehow angered the child. In her head she began repeating what the woman from Ontario had told her. "I kept saying, over and over, 'You are welcome to visit here, but now it's time to go to the light. Your mommy is waiting for you there.' I know it sounds far-fetched, but the voice just suddenly stopped, and since that day I have never heard it again. There has been nothing."

As for her home's connection to the orphanage where the little girl may have been abandoned by her mother, Nancy says at first she was confused by that since she knew the location where she and her husband had built their house had no link to any such facility. However, when she later learned that the home of the local contractor they had hired to build their house was located on property where an old orphanage had been many years earlier, she put it all together. "I believe that somehow the spirit of that little girl became attached to our carpenter, and when he came to work on our house, he brought the ghost with him. When he left, the little girl stayed with us," Nancy explains. "I really believe that."

*   *   *

In the Maritimes

• If the palm of your right hand itches, it means you are going to shake hands with a stranger.

• If the palm of your left hand itches, it means you are going to come into some money.

The Pink Ladies

Down through the centuries, ghosts have been reported in a variety of shapes and sizes. They've taken on the likeness of humans and animals and, typically, they haunt inanimate objects such as rocking chairs, mirrors, photos and old sea captains' trunks. But few ghosts have been reported to be of different colours. However, in a home somewhere on the south shore of Nova Scotia, two ghosts have taken on a decidedly different hue from most of their kind.

The story of the colourful spectres begins some 20 years ago when a young man, who shall be named Kirk to protect his identity, purchased a quaint home located in one of the small seaports hugging the rugged Nova Scotia coastline. It's a seaport made famous with tales of pirates, buried treasure and ghost ships. The home is believed to be about 200 years old and is one of five houses with a near identical appearance in the town. That could be because the homes were all built by the same man, but it's really the unearthly inhabitants that make Kirk's home unique.

Vicki, Kirk's wife, explains that her husband owned the home for about 10 years before the two met. "My husband is a straight and narrow man," she points out, stressing that he would never admit to believing in ghosts or anything of a supernatural nature. "He just barely believes in God, so there is no way he believes in ghosts and there is absolutely no way that he would ever believe that our small house was haunted. He just would never go for that."

When Vicki and Kirk were married, they decided that because their house was very small, it would require some extensive renovations, especially if they were going to have children. It wasn't long after the renovations were complete that Vicki learned she was expecting. "We were very excited at the thought of bringing our baby home to our newly renovated house," she recalls with bubbling enthusiasm. "The house really is wonderful," she continues, but pauses, as if searching for the right words to explain her next thought. "Don't get me wrong. I love the house and I love what we did to it. It's just that I never felt like we were ever alone there. It's difficult to explain, but I felt like there was always someone else with us. I always felt as though someone was watching me, and while I never felt frightened, it sometimes made me uneasy. I just felt like I always had to be on my guard. It was just the strangest thing."

When Trevor was born, Vicki and Kirk were ecstatic, but it wasn't long until his nighttime behaviour became worrisome. "We didn't think he was sick or anything like that. He was perfectly healthy, but he would behave oddly at night," says Vicki.

Although things seemed normal during the daytime, Vicki says the nights were an entirely different story. "He just didn't want to be in his room by himself. No matter what time we put him down, he'd fuss. This happened all the time and we had to remain in his bedroom with him until he fell asleep. As he got older, we had to read him his story and we'd lay with him for a few minutes and he'd go to sleep. It usually didn't take very long. No more than 10 minutes or so and he'd go to sleep. But you could never just say good night and then leave. He'd scream as if something was wrong. I know some people would say he was just spoiled, but it wasn't like that."

Once asleep, little Trevor rarely made it through the entire night. Vicki says, "He'd wake up in the middle of the night. He'd be screaming and crying and we always thought it was night terrors. We had heard about that before and we thought that's what it was. We know of other parents whose children behave like this, and they tell us it's a terrible experience for them and their children. When Trevor awoke, I'd go into his room and lay with him for a while, stroke his hair and try to comfort him by telling him that Mommy was there. Eventually, he'd go back to sleep. But this was every night. This wasn't just once in a while."

Vicki and Kirk were at odds about what to do for their son. "He was having a terrible time and it wasn't any picnic for us either." This went on for well over three years, she points out.

Then one night during one of these episodes, Vicki finally got a hint at what might be going on with Trevor, and although she didn't like the answer, she admits that in a way she was glad that she had something to work with. "One night when this happened and we went through this routine, I couldn't get him to calm down," Vicki explains. "I had seen him upset before, but this time, he was just hysterical and wouldn't stop crying. When I asked him what was wrong, he said, 'Tell those ladies to leave me alone.' I'm like, 'what?' He must be dreaming, I thought."

But Vicki says Trevor continued and she knew he was serious. "'Those pink ladies,' he cried. 'They won't leave me alone.' Of course, I'm thinking he's had a really bad dream or something. I asked him what happened."

To Vicki's amazement, Trevor said, "'Those pink ladies. They tickle me in my sleep and I don't like it. Make them stop, Mommy. Make them go away.'

"And I said, 'Isn't that silly. Why do they tickle you, Trevor?'

"And he continued crying. 'I don't know,' he sobbed. 'They always tickle me and won't leave me alone. They do it every night.'"

Hoping to soothe him, Vicki remained with her son for several hours until he finally fell asleep. The next day, after he had calmed down, she asked Trevor what was happening with these pink ladies in his room.

"And he said, 'Yes, Mommy. Every night, those pink ladies, they tickle me. Make them go away.'

"And I said, 'Trevor, you must be dreaming. There are no pink ladies in your room.'

"But he insisted. 'No, Mommy. They are there every night and they tickle me and I can't get them to stop.'"

Vicki pauses, collecting her thoughts before continuing the story. "I asked him what they looked like, and he said they were pink and they had grey legs. Up to this day, he will tell me about these pink ladies, and it's been a few years since he's seen them. Keep in mind that he was only three when he started talking about the pink ladies."

Of course, Vicki says, Kirk did not put much stock in Trevor's story. "He insists that the kid was dreaming, but I didn't think so. It seemed like more to it to me than just a dream. Trevor was really frightened to go to sleep in his room because he feared the pink ladies would come and tickle him."

While Vicki was prepared to accept that something extraordinary was happening in their home, Kirk would not even consider the possibility of a spirit or anything of that nature, so Vicki was at a loss as to how to handle the situation, and she knew better than to bring up the subject around her skeptical husband.

Time passed, but Trevor talked about the pink ladies all the time, and his night terrors persisted. "We even tried moving him into another room for a while, but that didn't help. We weren't getting much sleep in that house, I can tell you that."

All old homes come with the usual assortment of squeaks, cracks and creaks. People usually dismiss the noises as "settling," and as Vicki says, "You expect that all the time." But sometimes there is more to it than that.

About a year after Trevor first told his parents about the pink ladies, Kirk and Vicki were lying in bed. It was late. "We'd had a second son, Travis, by that time, and he was still an infant. Maybe we're overly cautious parents or paranoid or something like that, but when you've been going through what we were going through, you just take precautions. We had monitors in every room where the children could be. In their bedrooms and even their bathroom. One night, I'd say it was around two in the morning, my husband and I had just gone to bed and were laying there talking like we often did after a busy day. Suddenly, over the monitor from Trevor's bedroom we heard the doorknob turn and the door open. There is no doubt about what we heard. It was clearly the doorknob turning and the door opening."

Vicki says their first thought was that Trevor had gotten out of bed and was going into his brother's bedroom, as he often did in the morning. However, at this hour of the night, Vicki knew that if her eldest son made it to his brother's room and woke up Travis, then they would never get either child back to sleep. "Kirk quickly jumped up from bed and ran down the hallway to the boys' bedrooms," Vicki recalls, her trembling voice betraying her emotions. "He was gone a few minutes, but upon his return he was as white as a ghost. I thought something was wrong with one of the kids. I didn't know what to expect.

"'Vicki,' Kirk said. 'The boys are both sound asleep.'

"He looked at me. I looked at him, and we both knew something wasn't right. We both knew what we heard over the monitor, and there is no question we heard that door-knob turn and the door open. Both Kirk and I heard it, so we knew we weren't dreaming. From that point on, although he never liked to admit it, Kirk began to accept that maybe something wasn't right about our house. He never liked to talk about it, but I knew he now believed that we might not be alone in our home."

As the days went by, Vicki says she became more uncomfortable in her own home. "I knew we weren't alone, and although I didn't think the spirts or whatever it was would harm the children, I still didn't like being there. It made me uneasy. Then one day I told one of my good friends about what had happened, and she told me I needed someone to come into the house and do a cleansing or something like that. We needed to find out what was happening in our house, and then maybe we could get the spirits to leave. She told me she knew some people who could help, but I had to believe. I told her I did."

A few nights later, Vicki's friend brought over to the house a man and woman who Vicki had never met before. Without hesitating, the pair immediately made their way up to the second-floor bedrooms while Vicki, Kirk and their friend remained downstairs. "In all, I would say they were up there more than an hour. We had no idea what they were doing," Vicki recalls.

When the two clairvoyants returned to the group on the main level, Vicki remembers that the woman had been crying. It was clear the pair had encountered something very emotional while upstairs. The clairvoyants subsequently relayed their experiences from the second floor. Upon their arrival, the man and woman had split up and gone into each of the boys' rooms. In each of the rooms they discovered spirits crouching in a corner. Upon being discovered, the beings exited the boys' rooms, making their way to the master bedroom. There the clairvoyants managed to get readings from the spirits.

They told Vicki and Kirk that they could sense that the spirts were both women and were both very sad. They did not know why the spirits were sad, but they thought that something tragic had occurred in the 200-year-old house that affected these women, and they were tied to the property. Perhaps they had lost children in this house because they felt these spirits did not mean any harm to the children. They just wanted to be with them. Vicki says that is when she knew the pink ladies Trevor had been seeing were real.

After that, although Vicki says she never felt frightened in her home, she still did not feel comfortable. Eventually, they decided to sell their home and move into a larger house on the other side of town, but even that decision made Vicki feel uncomfortable because she didn't want the spirits to be angry that they were taking the children away. She didn't know how they would feel about that, and she feared the pink ladies might follow them to their new property.

Upon moving into their new home, Trevor's dreams and night terrors came to an abrupt stop, but he never forgot the pink ladies. Even though it's been years since they moved out, every time they drive past their old home with the children in the car, Trevor will remind his younger brother that they used to live there and, Vicki says, "he always adds…with the pink ladies."

*   *   *

In the Maritimes

• Should a bride or groom encounter an open grave on the way to or from their wedding, it is considered to be a foreboding symbol. In the Maritimes, many people believe it is best to avoid passing a cemetery on the way to the church.

The Haunted House
on the Cliff

If the word Pugwash sounds familiar, it could be because it is known around the world as a place of peace. The town dates from the mid-1700s, when New England colonists were lured to the area by land grants from the Nova Scotia government. Soon after the American Revolutionary War, United Empire Loyalists fled the United States to Canada. Then settlers from the British Isles arrived. Influenced by English pronunciation, the settlement's Mi'kmaq name, Pagwe'ak, became Pugwash. Although devastating fires razed the village several times, today Pugwash is known around the world because of the role it has played in the struggle for worldwide peace as the host of the Pugwash Conferences on Science and World Affairs.

Pugwash also has a place in the world of the paranormal; it's just not as well known. Perched high on a cliff at Lewis Head near Port Hope at Cameron's Beach, a place not far from Pugwash, sits a house that its owners say has more than its fair share of unearthly dwellers. The house wasn't built on its present cliff-side perch, where it is bordered by water on three sides. Although the home's history is shrouded in mystery, its owners describe it as a typical, two-storey farmhouse.

Julie Wamboldt, who lived there for 27 years, says the house was purchased by her husband's father and moved there from an unknown location. "That's about all we know about it," she says, explaining that by the time she and her husband began asking questions about the house's original location, her father-in-law had already died and taken whatever information there was to the grave with him. "We know the house is old, but that's about all we know. If something happened there, the secret remains hidden within its walls."

Although today Julie does not reside in the home, she still visits regularly because her daughter and family now live there. "I still get there a fair bit, but I haven't lived there for a few years." However, she adds, she still has vivid memories of the unusual activity that occurred at the house.

She does not hesitate when she says, matter-of-factly, that the house is haunted. "I knew right from the beginning that something wasn't quite right with the house. I couldn't explain it, but it was something I could feel. From the time I moved into that house with my husband, every night I could hear someone walking up the steps," she says, admitting that although she heard the ghost many times, she never actually saw it. "But I believed it was there. The first time I heard it, I remember hearing the ninth step creak—that could only happen if you walked on it—and I went right out and looked down, but there was no one there. There's no way that step could have creaked unless someone was on it." And Julie says she wasn't the only one who heard it. "The whole family heard it, and many different people who came to visit also heard it. It became a regular feature of the house."

But there was more evidence that the house contained a ghost, Julie quickly adds, explaining that at the top of the stairway, there is a large landing space where they kept a bed, and Julie's daughter slept there. The young girl was about nine when she had a ghostly encounter that has remained with her for her entire lifetime.

Beside the girl's bed was the doorway to a spare bedroom for unexpected visitors, as was customary in those days. "This was many years ago when my children were young, but one morning when my daughter got up, she said, 'Mom, where did you get that long, white dress?' I didn't know what she was talking about and I told her, 'I don't have any white dress.'"

Julie remembers being surprised by her daughter's response. "She said to me, 'Yes, you do. You had it on last night when you came and covered me over.' And then she asked what I was doing in the spare room last night because we never go in there, especially not at night. I wouldn't have any reason to go there, so I told her I wasn't in the spare room. My daughter swears to this very day that on that night she saw a woman wearing a long white dress in the spare room. First the woman came and tucked her in, and then she made her way into the room. For what, we don't know. My daughter thought it was me until I told her differently. And she swears that it wasn't a dream, but no one else ever saw anything like that."

However, there have been many other incidents over the years that have convinced Julie the house is, without a doubt, haunted. "One time, my sister and her husband and their young son were visiting us from Springhill. Downstairs, we had one room that had chairs that folded down to make beds. My sister and her husband were sleeping in one bed and the little boy was in another. During the night, my sister woke up when she heard footsteps in the dining room, which was right next to the room they were in. She thought it was her son roaming about, so she whispered for him to come back to bed before he woke everyone up. Immediately, she heard the footsteps come into the room and up to her bed. She then felt someone brush past the bed as if they were trying to feel their way in the dark. Thinking she would help her son get back to bed, my sister turned on the light and, to her surprise, her son was sound asleep in the other bed, and there was no one else in the room."

On another occasion, Julie's parents were visiting and stayed in the spare room. "My mother always took her clothes off and put them on the chair beside the bed. She did that all the time whenever they visited. One morning, to her surprise, when she got up and fetched her clothes, her stockings were missing. If I didn't know my mother's habits, I'd say she put them someplace else, but if my mother said she put her stockings on the chair, then I believe she put them there. Besides, things were always disappearing in that house. We just got used to it."

Throughout the years, Julie says, there were regular reports of unusual happenings in the house, particularly in the spare bedroom. "Many guests have told us there was something scary about the room, that they felt threatened to stay in there—some said it was just cold and they couldn't get warm—and over the years, many visitors told us of something trying to get into bed with them. Even though they could never see anything, we had many stories like that."

Today, Julie's daughter and her family live in the house and still occasionally experience things they cannot explain. Julie has never been able to find any answers about the property. "We still don't know much about the house, and after a while you just take it in stride. We just learned to accept that there was a ghost in our house. What else could we do?"

The Cuddling Ghost

To experience the cuddling ghost, one must travel to the small, picturesque hamlet of Dayspring, Nova Scotia. Nestled on the shores of the LaHave River, just a few kilometres outside of Bridgewater, Dayspring has strong ties with the shipbuilding and lumber industries. Today, few reminders of this proud heritage can be found, as modern technology has made that way of life all but obsolete. But in past centuries, Dayspring was a hub of activity.

Many of the homes in the sparsely populated community of Dayspring are of modest but practical design. Built to accommodate large families, the multi-level residences often housed more than one generation as the younger family members assumed responsibility for their elderly relatives. One such home is the Hirtle homestead. Built in 1906, the house has 11 rooms and has accommodated three generations of the Hirtle family. When Douglas and Noreen Hirtle got married in 1948, the couple moved into the house to take care of three of his relatives—Aunt Flow, Aunt Gladys and Uncle Harvey. In time, they had three children of their own—two sons and one daughter—and they all lived happily together for many years.

Although Noreen now lives alone in the expansive home, when Douglas died in 1977, she continued to raise her children and take care of the Hirtle relatives. But they've all gone now; her children are married with families of their own, and the relatives are long since deceased. The last remaining relative, Aunt Flow, died in 1994 at the age of 107. She had lived at the Hirtle homestead up to the age of 105, receiving

A ghost said to inhabit this home in Dayspring, Nova Scotia, likes to get close to its subjects.

tender loving care from Noreen until blindness made her care more demanding and she was forced into a nursing home. However, although her earthly family is now gone, Noreen is still not alone in the house. She says matter-of-factly, "I have company sometimes, it's just not the kind you'd expect."

She believes at least one ghost, if not two or maybe even more, share her home. Thinking back, Noreen believes the unseen visitors came to her home shortly after Douglas died in 1977. "I honestly can't remember anyone talking about anything unusual happening in the house before then, but when I think back to when things started happening, it seems to me it wasn't long after Douglas passed away."

Noreen's mother came to be with her fairly often after Douglas died, but because her age and resulting arthritis made it difficult for her to reach the bedrooms on the second floor, Noreen moved a bed into a small parlour just off the dining room. Whenever her mother visited, she slept there. Later on, Noreen even began sleeping there instead of going upstairs. "I remember it all started one day after my mother went home from one of her visits not too long after Douglas died. I was really tired and went into the parlour for a nap. I wasn't asleep long when I felt someone come into the room and sit on the edge of the bed. You know how it is when you're kind of half awake and half asleep? It's like you're not really sure about what's happening. Are you dreaming or are you awake? Well, that's what I was like. I then felt someone lie down next to me on the bed and put their arm around my waist."

Noreen says she may have been napping, but she's sure that by this time, she was awake. "At first, I thought it was one of my next-door neighbours playing a trick on me, but then I realized it wasn't. I realized there really wasn't anyone there in the room with me. I jumped up out of bed and looked around the room, but I was alone. I told myself I had been dreaming, but I knew I hadn't been. It was just the weirdest feeling. I could have sworn that someone had put their arm me and was cuddling up to my back. You can't imagine that. You can't know that feeling."

After that initial incident, Noreen experienced the cuddling ghost on several occasions when she slept in the bed in the parlour. "And each time, it was much like the first time. I'd feel someone lie down next to me, snuggle up really close and put their arm around me. But I wasn't frightened in any way. I never felt there was any reason be afraid. I really

Noreen Hirtle sits in the room of her home where she experienced her first encounter with the cuddling ghost.

didn't think he was crazy. How could I think he was crazy after what had been happening to me? The only difference was that this young fellow was staying in one of the upstairs bedrooms and I was in the parlour."

Noreen insists that before that evening, she had never told anyone about her experiences with the cuddling ghost. "I swear I never told a soul about it. I wouldn't want anyone to think I was crazy, but after I heard his story, I knew I wasn't crazy."

Her house guest told her he had gone to sleep the previous night, but he soon woke up when he felt someone get into bed with him, snuggle up close to him and up put their arm around him. "It was just like what had been happening to me. I will admit when I heard him talk about it, it gave me goose bumps because at that minute, I knew something had to be going on," Noreen says. "He told me he jumped up, turned on the lights and was surprised to see there was no one in the room with him. It left him pretty shaken up. He really didn't know what to think. I could see that it was really bothering him, so I finally told him what was happening to me. He couldn't believe it. I think that hearing about my experiences made him feel a little better to know he wasn't going crazy, but it still made him a little uneasy to think there might be a ghost wanting to get into bed and cuddle with him."

Other houseguests to the Hirtle homestead have had unusual experiences that defied explanation, but not all of them were as friendly in nature. "One of my grandsons was staying with me for a few nights. This was few years back now. He was sleeping in one of the upstairs rooms. We were having a great visit until one night when I woke up and found him standing in my room. I asked him if something was wrong, and I could tell he was terrified. Every night when he went to bed, my grandson had a habit of taking a glass of water with him. He'd set it on the floor beside the bed so he could reach it without getting up. Well, it seems on this particular night, when he reached down to get his glass of water, something reached out from under the bed and grabbed his hand. He said it held on to him for a long time and wouldn't let go. I could tell he was afraid. I told him he must have been dreaming but he said he hadn't been, and he would not go back to the room. I had to let him sleep with me for the remainder of the night."

Once, when another grandson was spending the night, the ghost or ghosts visited again. "This time, the next morning at breakfast, he told me that during the night, he woke up when he felt something get onto his bed. All of a sudden, he felt something crawl on top of him and sit on his chest. He said he tried to get it off, but it just kept pushing him down and it held him there for a while. It wouldn't let him get up. He said whatever it was just felt heavy on his chest. He told me he kicked and yelled until finally it let him go. He swears that he then heard something go out the bedroom door and run down the steps, but he hadn't seen anything. He said after that he was too scared to get out of bed, so he just stayed there until he heard me get up. I don't really know what happened to him that night. I didn't hear anything, but I can tell you it scared the daylights out of him."

Strange things seem to happen in the upstairs bedrooms, and Noreen says she can't explain it. "I had another guest staying in one of the rooms, and the next day she told me a story about someone lifting up the mattress and tucking her in. She swore that she could feel it. After everything else that had been going on in the bedrooms over the years, I believed her. Why wouldn't I?"

Over the years, stories from the bedrooms became fairly common, Noreen says. "I had a niece visiting once who also had an unusual encounter with something in an upstairs bedroom. It was between three and four in the morning when it happened. She said she was woken up when she felt someone lift her left arm up and slam it back down on the bed. She said it happened with so much force that it actually hurt. I don't know why it would want hurt to her that way.

It seems the younger people have the more violent experiences with whatever is in the house."

But some adults have also experienced the violent side of this ghost. "My sister and her daughter were visiting for a few days, and they were in an upstairs bedroom. They were sleeping in the same bed. On this one night, my sister got out of bed to go to the bathroom or get a drink of water or something. When she returned to bed a few minutes later, she moved closer to her daughter for warmth. Suddenly, she felt someone else get into bed with her, reach over and put their arm around her. Then she felt them, or it, put their weight on her legs and push down. My sister was terrified. She knew there was no one else in the room with them. She tried and tried to move her legs, but she just couldn't budge them. She told me that it must have lasted a few minutes, then suddenly the weight was gone and she could move again. I don't think she had ever heard the stories of the cuddling ghost, but she got most of it right. The only thing different from her experience and mine was the fact that she said she couldn't move her legs. I never experienced that."

Over the years, many other unusual things have happened in Noreen's house. "For instance, there was a time when I used to keep battery-operated Christmas candles on the mantle. One of those candles would turn off and on in the middle of the night even though there was no one around. I'd wake up and it would be on. Then later, it would be off. How could that happen? I thought maybe there was a bad connection or something like that with the switch, but I could never find anything wrong. The switch seemed to work just fine, yet the candle had a mind of its own."

As did the living room shades. "They'd go up on their own all the time. I'd pull them down and they'd go back up. I could never explain that one, but I just assumed it was one more strange thing in this house that had no explanation. So many people have experienced so many different things in this house over the years that after a while I've just grown to expect it and take it in stride. I never feel like I'm alone. So many people have passed through here and I have so many good memories. Even if there are ghosts in this house, I don't feel threatened by them."

Although Noreen believes the ghostly happenings started shortly after her husband's death, she in no way allows herself to think that it could be his ghost. There could be many explanations for the hauntings, she says. For one thing, one point of land not far from the Hirtle homestead is the location where, according to local legend, two natives were hanged for killing the family of an early white settler who had staked his claim at a place called Horseshoe Cove. Many local people believe the place is haunted. And just a few decades ago, a young girl was drowned in a nearby brook that runs close to Noreen's home, or so the story goes. Could the hauntings at the Hirtle home be connected to either of those two events?

Noreen isn't accepting those explanations either, however. "Some things just don't have an explanation," she reasons.

As for being afraid of whatever is in her house, Noreen asks, "What's there to be afraid of? If you wake up in the middle of the night and feel someone cuddling you, is that so bad? Maybe some people would be disturbed by the fact that there's not actually anyone there, but not me. Not after all these years."

Deadman Candles

Fredericton, the capital city of New Brunswick, is situated along the banks of the beautiful St. John River in the heart of the province. Graced with tree-lined streets, Victorian homes, top attractions, arts and cultural events, a variety of sporting facilities, kilometres of trails, acres of parks and green space, two universities and an airport, Fredericton is one of the most successful and vibrant small cities in North America, its website proudly proclaims.

In 1692, on behalf of the French king, Governor Villebon erected Fort Nashwaak to protect its French inhabitants. Then called Ste. Anne's Point, Fredericton was the capital of Acadia from 1692 to 1698. On February 22, 1785, Governor Thomas Carleton formally changed the town's name to "Fredericstown" in honour of Prince Frederick, Duke of York, second son of King George III. The name was quickly shortened to Fredericton.

Oscar Wilde once lectured in Fredericton's City Hall. Bliss Carman, Charles G.D. Roberts and Francis Joseph Sherman were all born and raised there, which is why Fredericton has been dubbed the Poets' Corner of Canada. The notorious Benedict Arnold once lived in Fredericton. His negotiations with the English were arranged by Jonathan Odell, a poet.

So one should not be surprised to discover ghosts and haunted houses among the stately properties of this city. Among those homes, some more than two centuries old, is one particular property where it is said the souls of long-passed inhabitants continue to haunt the hallowed hallways, oblivious, perhaps, to the reality of their own death. Over the years, the grand manor, with its richly decorated rooms and opulent furniture, has been owned by wealthy merchants and ship captains. In its heyday, the house was the scene of many elaborate social functions, with the city's elite and well-to-do gathering there to eat, drink and dance the night away.

Today, the manor is but a shell of its once-glorious self. Some witnesses say they have seen lights moving about and dancing or shimmering in the darkened windows of the vacant home. One of these witnesses, who wishes to remain anonymous because she says other people have either dismissed her reports as being hallucinations or merely a figment of her imagination, has firsthand knowledge of this strange phenomenon. In fact, the middle-aged woman insists she has seen these lights on more one than one occasion.

The woman says she believes the house, badly in need of some tender loving care, most notably a coat of paint, likely has many interesting secrets hidden away within its walls. She says this because she insists she has seen the spirits of those who once lived there. On at least four different occasions, the woman saw strange glowing lights emanating from the windows. Shaped sort of like orbs, the lights appeared to have been floating and gliding in midair because there was absolutely no one around.

The first time she saw the lights was over 10 years ago, she recalls, while she was walking her silky terrier as she does every evening. "It's our routine that every night, after supper and I get the dishes done and see to the kids' homework, I take Amber out for a walk," the woman says. "She loves going outside and we try to do it every day, no matter what it's like outside—sunny, rainy or snowing. She's only small, so taking her out in the middle of a major snowstorm can be a challenge, but we go anyway. Besides, it's good exercise for me as well."

It was during one of those snowstorms, in February 1997, that she saw the lights for the first time. "It was about 7:30, and it was dark and snowing pretty hard," the woman begins. "But Amber and I were trucking right along, just taking in the scenery. I'm one of those people who likes to look around when I'm out walking. Maybe I'm just nosey or something, but whenever I'm walking, I'm always glancing around, looking at people's yards and that sort of thing. I just like enjoying what's around me. Anyway, this evening, we weren't out any more than 10 minutes when we approached the house. It seemed darker and more drearier that night around that part of the neighbourhood. Maybe it was just the storm, but it just didn't seem right to me, and even Amber was a little timid to pass the house."

As she and her small dog drew closer to the cobblestone walkway that leads up to the main entrance of the manor, she caught a glimpse of something bright flickering in the darkened downstairs window of what would have been the parlour. "I know this sounds weird, but these lights were there. I'm sure there's no power going to that house anymore, but just as sure as I was standing there, there were two round, bright lights flickering inside that room. They were light yellowish-orange, and the weird thing about them was that although they were bright, they didn't seem to be casting any light from them. They were just glowing within themselves. And they were flitting back and forth as if playing with each other."

Remaining there for about five minutes, the woman watched the lights flicker and bounce around inside, but she is certain there was no one in the house. "If there had been anyone there, I'm sure I would have seen them."

Suddenly, the lights began to fade, then they were gone. "It was almost like they just went out. Like someone turned a switch off and the lights went dark. It was strange and sudden. I felt a little sad after that."

The first time she saw the lights, the woman did not tell anyone, not even her husband. "He doesn't believe in anything like this. He would have thought I was nuts, and if I hadn't seen [the lights] again a few months later, I might have thought that as well."

But she did see them again. About seven months after her first encounter with the lights, she and Amber were walking past the house around the same time as the previous sighting. It was a warm September evening, but the leaves were starting to change colour with the promise of fall. "The strange thing about this time was that it was still pretty light outside because the clock had not yet been turned back," she recalls, noting that as she passed the main walkway, she could see directly into the old parlour. She was startled to see the lights again. Only this time, she points out rather emphatically, there were more of them. "I don't know, maybe eight or nine of them. But they were all floating around inside the room and, I know this is weird, but it's like they were having a party. That's exactly how I felt when I saw them. It was just like when a group of people get together and have a party. I actually felt kind of warm and happy, unlike the first time I saw them."

When the woman returned home, she told her husband about the lights, and she admits his reaction was predictable. "He thought I was crazy. He told me no one has been in that house for years, so there's no way there could be lights in there, but I know what I saw. There were lights in there, and Amber knew it too because she barked and barked at them, but they didn't hear her."

It was about three years before the woman saw the lights again. This time, she saw the lights from one of the upstairs bedrooms. "There were only two lights this time, just like the first time," the woman says, "and they were bouncing around just like they had been before."

She still did not tell her husband about it. "I didn't want him to laugh at me again, even though I am 100 percent certain the lights were there."

The fourth and final time the woman saw the lights was in 2003. She now walks alone, having lost her beloved Amber in 2001. "I miss her companionship when I'm outside because I know how much she loved to walk, but I still try to walk every night. That night, it was February again and as I went past the house, I spotted the two lights in the parlour once again. I didn't stay long, but the lights continued to dance around. Even as I walked away, I could see them, and I watched the lights until I went out of eyesight."

Although she never told her husband about the additional sighting, she did relay her story to several friends, one of whom did some research into such phenomena. Her friend found out that such lights are very common in older homes or cemeteries where spirits are said to gather. In some cultures these lights are known as sprites or pixie lights, but they are more commonly known as deadman candles.

Sussex's Haunted Farmhouse

Sussex, a town in Kings County, New Brunswick, is located about 70 kilometres north-northeast of Saint John. In 1857, the European and North American Railway was opened, connecting the farming communities of the Kennebecasis River Valley with Saint John and Moncton. Sussex was incorporated in 1895 but was only officially established as a town on April 30, 1904. The settlers were, for the most part, descended from British Loyalists who had fled the American Revolution in 1776, with many Irish refugees of the potato famine of the mid-1800s settling in the nearby farming communities.

In 1885, the Sussex Military Camp was established on the eastern edge of the town. The facility was closed following World War II, and the town eventually purchased the land to expand municipal boundaries. Potash was subsequently discovered in large quantities in the area surrounding Sussex. The deposit was the second largest in the world behind an area in Saskatchewan, and two mines were built near the town.

Sussex also began to see a growing tourism trade, with many people flocking to see the collection of wooden covered bridges throughout the central area of Kings County. Today, the town is primarily a regional service centre for the surrounding agricultural communities of the upper Kennebecasis River Valley, as well as a highway service centre on Highway 1, the primary highway between Moncton and Saint John and the most heavily travelled route in the Maritimes to the United States.

Located on the outskirts of town on a rich tract of farm land sits a 12-room farmhouse that, according to its owners, is haunted. Although the owners request that the exact location of their property be kept secret, Barbara says without hesitation that over the years they have had many strange experiences that have led them to believe their home is the residence for more than just earthly beings.

"There's no doubt in our minds the place is haunted," begins Barbara. "I've always—ever since I was a little girl—had a strange feeling about the house. I knew there was something rather mysterious and very unusual about it, but not everyone believes in this sort of thing, and living in a small town such as Sussex, you have to be extremely careful about who you tell these things to, or else people will think there's something wrong with you. We've experienced that in the past when we've told people about our haunted house, and it's not very nice, so we're very mindful of what we tell people."

Barbara, who has lived in the farmhouse for more than 30 years, says that her first experiences with the ghost or ghosts began when she was very young, and things have escalated over the years with many other experiences. "But I remember it all started back one night when I was very young," she recalls. "I was only a little girl, maybe four or five at the time, and the room seemed very big to me. Anyway, it was getting late that night when it happened. I was in bed when I first heard it. It sounded like something was at my closet door. It was like someone was locked inside the closet and was trying very hard to get out. They were pushing and kicking and pounding on the door, but they couldn't get it open. The louder the noises became, the more afraid and upset I became. After a while, when the noises wouldn't stop, I called for my father. He came to my room and checked out the closet and told me everything was fine. He said he couldn't find anything there and that I should just go to bed and try to forget about it."

Barbara says the noises in her closet bothered her for a long time, and she hated going to bed for fear the noises would return or, worse still, that whatever had been trying out get out of the closet might actually get out one night. "My father never really liked to talk about the sounds in the closet all that much, but years later when I was discussing it with my mother, she told me that he was very disturbed about what had happened that night. It really bothered him that he couldn't find an explanation for what I had heard. He wanted to put my mind at ease, but he never could."

Over the years, other strange occurrences, such as hearing footsteps when there's no one else around, severe temperature fluctuations and feeling a presence in the house when you're all alone, have led the family to conclude that there is at least one ghost in their house. For instance, Barbara says matter-of-factly, "When you're alone in the house, you hear music playing but you can never find out where it's coming from." She says the soft, mellow music is very old-sounding, and it is as though a radio is playing in another room. "Only when you go to that other room, there's never any music there. Actually, it seems to move to a different room. You can try to find where it's coming from, but I can tell you, you never will."

Barbara has heard the music often, and she has actually followed it throughout the house, but she has never been able to find its origin. "In a way, the music is kind of soothing, but it's also kind of creepy that we can't find where it's coming from. Just imagine what it would be like to hear music playing in your house without being able to find its source. It's a weird thing."

Once, Barbara saw the image of a female form hovering in one of the upstairs rooms. "I've only ever seen it once, but that was enough for me. It was clearly a woman, and she was wearing a long black dress with a black shawl wrapped around her shoulders. I have no idea who the woman was, but it left me feeling pretty shaken for a long time."

Other than the image Barbara witnessed that one time, she says as far she knows, no one else has ever witnessed a form in the house. "The ghosts in our house don't seem to like to take the form of people." Instead, she adds, they take the form of mysterious lights or orbs. "Several times, both Mother and I have seen beams of multi-coloured light in the house when there is never any logical explanation for where they come from. I also once watched an orb of multi-coloured light as it floated up the stairway. It went up, and I followed it, then it just disappeared. I have no idea what it was or where it went."

Despite all these unexplained experiences, Barbara says she and her family have never really felt threatened in their home. "The house has been in my immediate family for almost 60 years, and nothing has ever happened there to make us feel we were in any kind of danger. Oh, it is sometimes unnerving to have these things happen right in front of your eyes, but that doesn't mean you are in danger. None of us has ever felt that way."

Over the years, the family has tried to discover the history of the house, which they estimate to be well over 200 years old. "We suspect it goes back to around the time of the War of Independence in the United States around 1776. Sussex became a major attraction for those people wanting to escape the war and for anyone wanting to farm. Other than that, there's not a whole lot we know about the place."

If some tragic event occurred on their property, Barbara agrees that might explain why their house is now haunted. "I think it's safe to say that whatever or whoever is in our house with us is most likely a former owner or at least a former inhabitant. You just get the feeling that these ghosts are at home, and since they don't bother us in any major way, we don't mind sharing it with them. What choice do we have?"

3
Ghostly
Local
Legends

Haunted Halifax

Governor Edward Cornwallis and 2500 settlers created Halifax, Canada's first permanent British town, in 1749 on the scenic shores of the world's second-largest natural harbour. Andy Smith operates Tattle Tours, a Halifax-based company that offers ghost walks and walking tours of historic Halifax as well as "step-on" guided tour services. Andy, also a professional actor and dialect coach, loves to tell ghost stories such as the following.

When the first Europeans set foot in what is now Nova Scotia more than 300 years ago, their arrival changed the course of life for the indigenous inhabitants of this land. Never would their existence be the same. As settlements grew, European and First Nations cultures clashed. Historic records tell the tale of two peoples trying to coexist in a place where only one had lived and prospered for generations. It was a land rich in natural resources, but still very rugged and raw, and it carried the promise of wealth and prosperity.

Going back in time to the early days of Halifax and the area around Halifax harbour, we find the story of one Mi'kmaq chief who, having lost one of his daughters to the European traders, decided to take matters into his own hands. When he learned that his daughter had been taken aboard a vessel that had sailed off back to Britain, the chief was furious, so he put a curse on the land. He predicted that three things would happen there over time. The first, he said, would be very violent. The second would be rather quiet, and the third would be long lasting.

Now, Andy says, in the late 1800s, they built the first bridge, a wooden walkway, across the span from what is now Halifax on one side of the harbour to Dartmouth on the other. It was up for a short time until a violent winter storm brought it crashing down. A few years later, the settlers replaced it with a railway bridge. It was up for some time; then, on a very quiet, calm summer evening, it fell. There was no explanation for its collapse.

In 1955, when the MacDonald Bridge was being built, the builders were smart enough to ask the current Mi'kmaq chief to come dispel the curse, pacify the area and bring peace to the land. The chief came and chanted a few chants and literally buried a hatchet to bring peace to the area. That bridge is still standing today.

Tour guide Andy Smith says one of the more interesting legends in Halifax is that which surrounds the construction of the MacDonald Bridge spanning Halifax Harbour.

Even more intriguing than that story is the tale of a little-known piece of joint Canadian-American history. Located in the centre of the city at the corner of Spring Garden Road and Barrington Street is the Old Burying Ground, the oldest cemetery in Halifax and a national historic site. Used by all denominations, the Old Burying Ground served the early settlers of Halifax from 1749 until its closure in 1844. It is estimated that there are somewhere in the vicinity of 1200 head- and footstones within the burying ground, but some historians suggest there are more than 10,000 people buried there because in the early days of settlement, the city suffered through epidemics of both typhoid and yellow fever. With so many people dying so quickly, the bodies had to be disposed of immediately. There was little time for fancy, expensive funerals. Besides, many of the thousands believed to be buried there were poor and could not afford an elaborate sendoff to the afterworld, let alone a costly grave marker. In fact, the Halifax debtors' prison was close by, which made the cemetery a convenient place to dispose of its deceased.

Within the Old Burying Ground, there is a section set aside for the military. At that location are crypts, raised graves and fancy monuments dedicated to the brave souls that rest there. One of those graves is the final resting place of Major-General Robert Ross.

Robert Ross was a British army officer who participated in both the Napoleonic Wars and the War of 1812. He was born in Rostrevor, County Down, now Northern Ireland. After the defeat of Napoleon, Ross sailed to North America as a major-general to take charge of all British troops on the east coast, taking up a post in Halifax. After the Americans made a daring raid in Toronto, then known as York,

Andy says the Old Burying Ground in the centre of Halifax holds a fascinating mystery.

during which the invaders burned several government buildings, Ross was sent to lead the British troops in the attack on the Americans at the Battle of Bladensburg on August 24, 1814. There, the American army of mostly militia quickly collapsed. Moving on from Bladensburg, Ross captured Washington, D.C. with little resistance. He insisted on only destroying public property, including the U.S. Capitol and the White House.

Based on that success, Ross organized an attack on Baltimore, Maryland. His troops landed at the southern tip of the Patapsco Neck peninsula at North Point, 20 kilometres from the city, on the morning of September 12, 1814. During the march, and just prior to the Battle of North Point, the British troops encountered American skirmishers, and Ross rode forward to direct his troops. An American sniper shot him through the right arm into the chest. According to Baltimore tradition, two American riflemen, teenagers Daniel Wells and Henry McComas, aged 18 and 19 respectively, were credited with killing Ross. Both young men were killed in the engagement. Ross died while being transported back to the ships.

After his death, the general's body was stored in a barrel of 129 gallons of good Jamaican rum and shipped on the British ship HMS *Royal Oak* to Halifax, where he was buried on September 29, 1814.

But the story doesn't end there. Indeed, it is just the beginning for those who believe in tales of the paranormal. Andy points out that many witnesses have claimed to see the ghost of Major-General Robert Ross roaming through the Old Burial Ground, his sword drawn for battle as if he is rallying the troops to move on to the next American city.

The Ghosts of Georges Island

It has been said that no matter where you go in Nova Scotia, the ghosts of its past are no more than a stone's throw away. That is certainly true with Georges Island, a small mass of land at the mouth of Halifax Harbour. Over the span of three centuries, spirits have been encountered on Georges Island with such frequency that, during the 19th century, this small drumlin was known as the most haunted place, for its size, in the entire province.

Dianne Marshall is considered the definitive authority on the ghosts of Georges Island. A native of Halifax, Dianne has always had a keen interest in its history and heritage. She has been a board member of the Heritage Trust of Nova Scotia and currently sits as a member of the Heritage Advisory Committee for the Halifax Regional Municipality. In 2003, Dianne published her first book on Halifax. It was titled *Georges Island: The Keep of Halifax Harbour*. Like many of us, she is fascinated by ghost stories and was more than happy to contribute these stories about the ghosts of Georges Island.

For more than 200 years, it has been widely believed that in the hours before dawn, when a hush descends over the harbour, the spirits of soldiers, pirates and a wide variety of scoundrels slip through a mysterious tunnel stretching across to Halifax to torment the nights of old sailors, or simply to join the dead of the town at the site of an old tavern near the waterfront for a mug of invisible ale and the company of a ghostly lass. These spirited fellows, however, share the island with a number of other apparitions.

THE LADY IN GREY

Sightings of the Lady in Grey were first reported in the latter part of the 18th century. Her clothing clings to her as though wet, and seaweed is tangled in her long blonde hair, but it is her eyes that make the most impact; in them, there is such despair that all who have met her—from the war-hardened soldiers of the Napoleonic era to modern visitors—have been struck with pity for her. The Lady in Grey paces back and forth along the rocky shore facing Dartmouth, as if desperately searching for a loved one.

Some people assume her to be the victim of a shipwreck, separated in death from a lover or child who went to the bottom of the harbour while her body was washed up on Georges Island. Others believe she is the lost spirit of a woman who took her own life by walking into the water following her soldier lover's execution for desertion on a nearby gallows. Whatever the true circumstances of her despair, anyone who has come across the Lady in Grey has never forgotten the experience.

THE DUC D'ANVILLE

Stories of other island spirits date back as far as 1749. According to local tradition, when the first settlers arrived with Governor Cornwallis, they were met by the disturbing sight of hundreds of skeletons dressed in tattered French uniforms and clutching rusted muskets, lying on beaches and leaning against trees around the harbour. These unfortunate men were the remains of the ill-fated French fleet led to

Chebucto a few years earlier by the duc d'Anville. Having contracted typhus during a long and difficult crossing from France, many hundreds died after their arrival—so many in fact, that there were not enough men to sail all of the ships back to France, and it became necessary to scuttle several in the harbour to prevent them from falling into enemy hands. D'Anville himself met a suspicious end shortly after their arrival. It was suspected that he had been poisoned—either by his own hand, or by one or more of his officers. He was buried on Georges Island, with little in the way of ceremony, at daybreak on September 17, 1746.

Within months of the arrival of the Cornwallis expedition, a party of French soldiers arrived via ship, with the governor's permission, to remove the remains of the duc d'Anville from his island grave and transport him to Louisbourg, where he was reburied in French soil. For the island's inhabitants, however, that was not the end of d'Anville's story, for though his grave had been emptied, it appeared that his spirit had remained behind.

At night, when most people were lying exhausted in their tents after a day of clearing trees and constructing log huts along the narrow streets of the new town of Halifax, others noted the occasional appearance on the beach of a fellow dressed in the uniform of a French admiral. When approached, he simply walked into the deep water and disappeared. It was an experience that was repeated over and over again for countless Haligonians over the next 150 years. After entering the water from the island's beach, the spirit would soon be seen emerging on the Halifax side. Curious locals would follow at a safe distance and watch as it made the trek along the shoreline until arriving at the Rockingham

Road. There, at a beach known locally as French Landing, the ghost would make a sharp right turn, march straight into the water and disappear.

Whenever the ghost walked, people living near the shore would report that they heard the creaking of invisible wooden ships and the sound of sails flapping in the night breeze. Because this was the place where a makeshift hospital of sails and spars had been set up to care for the dying men of d'Anville's fleet, it was assumed that the spirit was searching for his lost men and ships.

Reports of the admiral's walk were so frequent that in the late 19th century, the government commissioned a scientific investigation into the matter, though no adequate explanation was ever found. The exact location of the scuttled ships of d'Anville's fleet remained a mystery until the latter part of the 20th century, when they were discovered at last—in the water of the Bedford Basin directly opposite French Landing, where the ghost was seen walking into the water.

THE BURIAL PARTY

In the early part of the 19th century, a worker by the name of Drake, said to have been a descendent of the great British admiral Sir Francis Drake, was living in Halifax and was employed as a labourer on Georges Island. Shortly before dawn on a morning in mid-September, Drake arrived at the island to begin his workday and saw a sight that shook him to his very bones. He had just pulled his small craft up onto the beach and was climbing a path up the hill that would take him to the fort when he heard the familiar sound of oars hitting the water. He ducked behind some shrubbery and watched as a boat carrying six men approached the beach.

Once they reached shore, four men dressed in fine but ancient-looking uniforms stepped out and stood watching as the other two, who appeared to be ordinary seamen and were dressed more plainly, dragged the boat up onto the beach. From his position overlooking the scene, Drake could see something draped in cloth lying in the bottom of the boat. The two sailors reached in to retrieve shovels and, at a point selected by the other four, began to dig. Drake later remarked that not one of the men spoke a single word, and in the early morning light, all appeared to have very pale bluish faces.

When the men had finished digging a fairly deep hole, they stood leaning on their shovels while the officers returned to the boat to retrieve the object lying at its bottom. They carried what was clearly a man's body wrapped in dark velvet cloth and walked slowly toward the hole, which by now Drake had determined was a grave, and gently lowered the body into it. There was little ceremony to speak of, though after quickly covering the grave over with soil, all made a hasty sign of the cross—which to Drake's mind identified them as French—then returned to the boat and rowed away. As soon as they set off, Drake ran to the beach to investigate and found that the soil over the gravesite that he saw opened with his own eyes showed no signs of having been disturbed at all, and the boat carrying the burial party had vanished. There was no doubt in his mind that he had been watching a ghostly replay of the burial of the duc d'Anville.

THE ONE-ARMED MAN

In the early days of Halifax, Georges Island was almost completely covered with forest. Of those men who spent their nights in tents near the beach, few were inclined to venture through the trees to the southern tip, but several of those who did reported encountering a one-armed French soldier sitting on a rock and staring out to sea, as if waiting to be rescued. Because he did not respond when spoken to and quickly vanished when approached, many observers believed him to be the spirit of a man who had been either accidentally or intentionally left behind when what was left of the d'Anville fleet sailed out of the harbour and returned to France.

Throughout the 19th and 20th centuries, startled visitors reported being followed or observed by a one-armed man dressed in the clothing of an ancient soldier. Although he seemed curious about what they were doing, the fellow quickly disappeared when spoken to. The one-armed man may still be waiting on Georges Island for passage home to France.

*   *   *

In the late 19th century, there were so many spirits on Georges Island that a burial ceremony was conducted by a local clergyman in an effort to put them to rest once and for all. It appears to have had no effect whatsoever.

The Lady on the Lake

Darling Lake is located on the Evangeline Trail, which is actually the main highway route No.1, 15 kilometres northeast of the old seaport town of Yarmouth, Nova Scotia. The lake is named after Colonel Michael Ashley Darling, who, in the late 18th century, was sent to Yarmouth to inspect the newly formed militia stationed there. The young colonel was so impressed with the beauty and peacefulness of the spot that he named it Darling Lake.

A lady in white has been seen over the years at Darling Lake in Nova Scotia.

Today, the lake is known to those who study the paranormal because of its strategic location in Nova Scotia. Bob Benson, the owner and operator of the Churchill Mansion Inn, which sits high on a hill overlooking the picturesque lake, explains that a mathematically devised pattern of lines is spread out across the province of Nova Scotia. These "lay lines" have been of great interest to many researchers and authors who theorize that an unusual amount of energy can be detected where the lines intersect. Points of intersection include the communities of New Ross, Mount Uniacke and McGowan Lake, all places where unusual paranormal experiences are known to have occurred over the years. Like these other places, a vortex is located around Darling Lake, and Bob believes that explains the ghostly phenomena experienced there. "These stories of a woman being seen on and around the lake go way back," Bob says. "There have been many reports of the Lady on the Lake, but although I've heard them, I've never seen her myself. But I can tell you, people who have said they've seen her really believe that something is there."

One of the most believable stories Bob has heard over the years came from two men he had known for some time. It happened several years ago, in the mid-1990s, at about 2:30 early one morning when they were heading back to Yarmouth. "These two were driving in a truck heading in the direction of Yarmouth. All of a sudden, as they came around a corner near the lake, they both saw a young woman with long, flowing white hair wearing a long, white dress and standing in the middle of the road. The driver slammed on the brakes, but the vehicle couldn't stop in time and plowed into the woman. Both men thought they had run into the woman and were afraid that they had killed her."

Grabbing flashlights, Bob's two friends got out of the truck and searched around both sides of the road, looking for the woman they were sure they had just run over, but they couldn't find anything. "It shook those guys up pretty good. They were both convinced that they had seen this mysterious young woman, and they both insisted that they had run into her with the truck, but they were never able to find her."

Two years later, Bob says, the man who was driving the truck at the time of the first incident reported seeing the woman again as he was passing the lake. "This time he saw her near the lake, and he knew it was the same woman because she was dressed in a long white dress and had long hair. By the time he got the truck stopped and got out, she was gone. After that, he was convinced the lake was haunted."

Bob too became convinced the lake is haunted after a psychic staying at his inn several years ago asked if he knew who the woman was. "I had no idea what she was talking about," Bob says. "We were sitting in the living room area, and from there you can see the lake. The woman looked right past me over my shoulder and asked if I knew who the woman was.

"'Woman?' I asked. 'What woman?'

"'The woman standing out there on the lake,' she answered."

Bob admits he was shocked. He had heard the stories of the Lady on the Lake, but here was someone right in front of him saying she could see the ghost. He asked his guest to describe what she was seeing. "She told me she could see a woman with long hair wearing a long, flowing white dress standing in the middle of the lake. She described pretty much what my friends had described a few years earlier."

Coincidence? Bob doesn't think so. There is no way this woman could have known what the two men had seen several years earlier.

*   *   *

In the Maritimes

• Taking a woman on board a boat is considered bad luck.

• Knocking over a salt shaker is considered bad luck.

New Glasgow Spirits

New Glasgow, a picturesque town situated along the banks of the gently flowing East River, is just minutes away from the beautiful waters of the Northumberland Strait. With a population of close to 10,000 residents, New Glasgow is the largest town in Pictou County in Nova Scotia. The town's early beginnings and prosperity are entwined with the development of the scenic East River, a tidal estuary of salt water and fresh water, and there is no doubt that the charm of the river drew the Scots to the area. The community that was to become New Glasgow was settled in 1784 when Deacon Thomas Fraser built on land that is now the west side of the town. By 1809, the town had been named after Old Glasgow in Scotland, and it was officially incorporated in 1875. Today, efforts are underway to revitalize the riverfront and bring it back to the glory days of the 19th century, when New Glasgow had a thriving shipbuilding industry.

New Glasgow is the birthplace of George MacKenzie, known as the father of Nova Scotia shipbuilding. Captain MacKenzie established a shipbuilding business in New Glasgow in 1840, and during his lifetime built or owned 34 vessels. When he withdrew from the business, it was taken over by his nephew, James William Carmichael. The Carmichael-Stewart House Museum, located on Temperance Street, is a stately Victorian structure that pays tribute to the shipbuilding heritage of the region. Hundreds of ships were built along New Glasgow's East River.

The waterways that have played such a vital role in the history of New Glasgow have spawned their fair share of local mysteries and legends as well as one or two ghost stories. Lynn MacLean, a former elementary school teacher who lives in New Glasgow, owns and operates Living History Tours. The small company provides fun and informative Ships and Spirits tours. "People are drawn to these things. They seem to love to be scared for some reason," Lynn says.

One of the more popular stories her guides relate during the tour is that of the ill-fated cargo ship *Melmerby* and the location where she subsequently ran aground, a mysterious place known as Melmerby Beach. Lynn describes Melmerby Beach as a place of tragedy dating back centuries. "On this beach, for some reason, there have been many, many accidents and a lot of deaths. It's really no wonder that people say it's haunted," she says.

Lynn points out, for example, that on November 21, 1850, there were three shipwrecks, all within 100 metres of each other. "That seems like more than just coincidence," she says, adding that only two days before this interview in early September 2006, another tragedy had befallen the area when a young woman drowned there. "It just seems that throughout the history of this area, there is ongoing reference to the tragedies at Melmerby Beach. It's a sad place."

One of the best known stories of death and destruction that involves the beach is the wreck of the *Melmerby*, a supply ship that sailed out of Quebec in late September 1890 with a cargo of timber. On October 1, approximately five days after leaving Quebec, the *Melmerby* encountered severe weather. In spite of the crew working the pumps, *Melmerby* was in danger of foundering. The order was given to jettison the deck load, but before the crew could accomplish this, the timber got out of control and smashed three of the four lifeboats. After eight days of foundering, the schooner *Mary* happened upon the troubled *Melmerby*, and *Mary's* captain came aboard to attempt to help guide the *Melmerby* to Pictou. Shortly after that, another storm overtook both vessels, and they were separated.

Melmerby subsequently lost her mast and was driven aground near New Glasgow. Sixteen men boarded the remaining lifeboat and made for shore. The lifeboat overturned in the fierce waters, and all but one person drowned. Locals who had gathered on the shore formed a human chain and managed to reach the one survivor in the water. Two days later, two of the six crew remaining on the *Melmerby* decided to swim for shore. Again a human chain of onlookers helped to pull them from the water. The *Melmerby's* lifeboat was repaired and used to rescue the remaining four who were left on board, including the captain of the *Mary*. The wreck remained visible long enough for the beach to be named Melmerby. Today, Lynn says, when weather conditions are just right, you can see the crippled *Melmerby* foundering just offshore from the beach, and if you listen, you can sometimes hear the screams of the crew as they succumb to the dark, wet depths of the Northumberland Strait.

Like the strait, the town's famed East River has its share of mysteries. Lynn explains that during the height of the shipbuilding activity on the river, the waterway had to be dredged regularly to allow ships to pass through unencumbered. Shipbuilding was an integral part of New Glasgow's infrastructure from 1798 to 1908, but then the activity pretty much dried up. "However, during that busy period, they dredged the river many times and to help do that, they often brought in foreign crews, mostly from the Orient," she says.

"During one of these times, a group arrived in New Glasgow from the Orient and of those, only one of them was able to speak English. He acted as their spokesperson. He would collect the crewmembers' pay and distribute it."

One time following a payday, this English-speaking worker disappeared. "No one could find him," Lynn explains. "His co-workers didn't know where he was, and his employers had not seen him since he collected the pay. No one could figure out what would have happened to this guy and no one ever found him—or at least, no one ever found him alive. Over the next few days, the remaining crew from the Orient moved out of town and went west, and the people of New Glasgow never saw them again. However, a few days after the group's departure, the headless body of a man was found floating in the East River. His hands were tied behind his back, and he was wearing the same type of clothing that the Oriental crewmen had worn. It was assumed that the body was that of the group's spokesman and that perhaps he was cheating the men out of some of their pay, and they found out about it. The locals concluded the group had done him in and then left town."

In time, the people of New Glasgow forgot all about the missing man from the Orient who had supposedly lost his head, but on certain evenings, when the moon is full, you can still see a headless body floating in the river.

Another intriguing New Glasgow mystery has nothing to do with water, Lynn explains, but it does date back to the town's early years. On February 18, 1880, a young woman named Marie Murray, who lived in the nearby town of Trenton, gave birth to five babies—two boys and three girls. They were the first quintuplets born in Canada. Multiple births were an unusual occurrence back in those days before fertility drugs, so interest in the Murray quintuplets was widespread. However, the lack of modern medicine also meant the babies' chances of survival were not good. Within the first day, three of the babies had died. The fourth baby died the following day, and the fifth baby died on the fifth day after his birth.

According to health records, the babies had each weighed around three pounds, but physically, they were said to be in good shape. As word of the quintuplets spread, a photographer arrived at the Murray home on the fourth day to take their picture. By this time, all but one of the babies had died. Still, they lined up the babies on a blanket and took the photo. Once the picture hit the news wire services, it was seen by P.T. Barnum of the renowned Barnum and Bailey Circus. He contacted the Murray family and asked them if he could buy their babies to put on display in his circus.

Of course, the family refused, but the story goes that Barnum gave them a hard time and tried to pressure them into selling the babies. The family so feared the famed circus man that they were afraid to bury the babies in a cemetery because they believed someone might dig them up and sell them. To protect the babies, the family buried them in the basement of their home, where the bodies remained for two or three months. Eventually, a prominent New Glasgow resident, whose identity remains secret to this day, offered to hide the babies in his family plot. The exact location of that gravesite has never been revealed. Not even the family could visit the plot because their presence in any of the local cemeteries would have revealed the location of the babies.

Today, Lynn says, some people believe the babies are buried in Riverside Cemetery in New Glasgow and that on certain nights as you're strolling through the graveyard, if you listen very carefully, you can hear the gentle sounds of five babies crying as if calling for their mother or someone to come find them.

While Lynn admits that she has never personally experienced any of these mysterious phenomena firsthand, she notes that it is interesting that each of them seems to have some basis in actual events. Is Melmerby Beach haunted by the ghosts of the crew members who perished on the ill-fated cargo ship? Does the headless body of an Oriental harbour worker float in the East River? Can you hear the cries of five long-lost babies in a local cemetery? Perhaps.

Ghosts of the Strait

The Northumberland Strait, a tidal water body between Prince Edward Island and the coast of eastern New Brunswick and northern Nova Scotia, extends 225 kilometres west-northwest to east-southeast from Cap-Lumière, New Brunswick, to Cape George, Nova Scotia. It is 4 to 17 kilometres wide and 68 metres deep at its eastern end but less than 20 metres deep over a large central area. Geographically speaking, the Northumberland Strait is a natural wonder. Supernaturally speaking, it is a place of wonderment. The coastal communities that border the Northumberland Strait have long registered a variety of paranormal activity. Stories of haunted houses, ghost ships and buried treasure guarded by the spirits of bloodthirsty buccaneers are mainstays of many local legends. One of the most popular and well-known stories is that of the burning ship of the strait. The story goes back several centuries to when a large, two-masted ship caught fire out on the strait. It was a tragedy. People were burned or drowned when they tried to swim to shore.

Joan LeBlanc is a writer and freelance journalist who lives in a small, rural community called Woodside. With a population of no more than five, the tiny settlement is located near Port Elgin, New Brunswick, which is not far from the university town of Sackville. It is practically a stone's throw from the Nova Scotia border and about 15 minutes from the Confederation Bridge, which links Prince Edward Island to the mainland. Joan says she has heard many of these local legends and agrees that they sometimes take on a life of their own. However, these stories are part of the community's fabric and, she adds, they're what make the region unique and contribute to its personality.

"The ghost ship of the Northumberland Strait really is the standard story of a ship on fire," Joan says. "However, for those who have seen it firsthand, it is very real. I know a woman, she's about 70 now, who insists that she actually saw the burning ship, and she is adamant about that. It was many years ago. This woman lived in an older home built on a piece of property that abutted right onto the Northumberland Strait. She says it was Christmas Eve the night she saw the burning ship. It was very, very late, and as she happened to look out her kitchen window and across the strait, there it was, burning brightly out on the water. Of course, it was in the middle of winter and there was ice in the strait. She knew this could not be any ordinary ship. This woman says she could see people jumping and screaming and could hear a great deal of noise. She also remembers that the fire was very bright—unnaturally bright. She knew that it was the ghost ship. What else could it be?"

Joan next tells the story of two young men from the Pugwash area of Nova Scotia who saw the ship one night, and they were never the same again. "Apparently, the two young men were coming off a night of revelry and were walking home along the shore, just having a good time, when they saw a burning ship out on the water. They were very concerned for the safety of the people on board because the fire looked really bad. It seems they had never heard the stories of the mysterious burning ship. The two men hurried down the shore to a little dock that they knew was there. Once at the dock, they got into a small boat and started rowing toward the burning vessel. They rowed and rowed until they thought they should have reached the ship, but it was gone. It was nowhere to be seen. When they turned around to look back to shore, there it was—behind them. Somehow, the two young men had rowed right through the burning ship." Needless to say, Joan points out, the men didn't take the same route back to shore.

But the haunted ship of the Northumberland Strait isn't the only ghost story from this region of New Brunswick. Joan says the area is ripe with them. "I know this one gentleman who tells the story of an incident many years ago when he was 15 or 16. As young boys of that age often do, this fellow and some of his friends had been in Baie Vert, which is near Port Elgin, for a Friday night of fun. They were out playing cards and having a few drinks at a friend's house. When it got late, he and some friends decided they were going to stay overnight at an old abandoned home just down the road from where they were partying. The house belonged to the uncle of one of the boys, so they figured it would be all right for them to stay there. They were sure the uncle wouldn't mind."

It was late, and as the young fellows were walking toward the house, they looked up and saw light in one of the windows on the top floor. They knew the house was not occupied, and there was no electricity running to it, so they couldn't determine where the light was coming from, but they decided they would stay there anyway because they were a ways from home and everyone was tired. "No one felt like walking home, so they went inside and went right upstairs to the bedrooms. Even though no one had lived there for a while, some of the furniture been left behind, including a couple of cots," Joan explains. "Well, no sooner had the fellows crawled into bed, pulled the blankets up and got their eyes closed, then they all of a sudden heard this terrible roar accompanied by a series of loud smashing and banging sounds. They said it was terrifying. They were out of bed and downstairs in just a matter of seconds to see what was going on. They were thinking that some of their friends had followed them and now were up to no good. Upon inspection, however, the fellows found that all the doors and windows were still locked tight, but there were pots and pans all over the kitchen floor. How they got there they didn't know, but obviously someone had been making noises with the pots."

After double checking the main floor of the house, the boys went back upstairs, but the noises happened several more times until the young men decided they should just leave. "As they walked away from the house, they could see the light from the upstairs window again, but they knew there was no logical explanation for it. They said it felt like something was watching them from the window. They couldn't explain it, but they felt there was something there. Perhaps that's why the place had been empty for so long. There had been stories going around the town there was something in the house, and I guess maybe that's why people hadn't lived in it."

Baie Vert, which means "green bay" in French, is a very old community, Joan says, so stories like that are fairly common. "There is documentation to prove that people arrived there in the 1500s, and along with that, there were all kinds of stories that the famous pirate, Captain Kidd, buried his stolen treasure around these parts.

"In Baie Vert, there is a stately old house—and it's still there today—that is said to have a secret. When the house

The Phantom Ship of Baie des Chaleurs

Bathurst is a city in northeastern New Brunswick located at the mouth of the Nepisiguit River on the Baie des Chaleurs in Gloucester County. The first Europeans to settle the area were the Acadians, but other early settlers included English, Irish and Scottish immigrants. The city of Bathurst was named in honour of Henry Bathurst, 3rd Earl Bathurst (1762–1834), Secretary of State for the Colonies of the British government. Construction of the Intercolonial Railway of Canada in the mid-1800s connected the port of Bathurst to the rest of the world and became an essential element for shipping products of the city's principal industries: forestry and zinc mining. And for those people interested in the paranormal, Bathurst is home to one of the greatest legends in Maritime folklore.

It is said that the phantom ship of Baie des Chaleurs, as it is called by the locals, haunts the waters off the shores of Bathurst. Legend tells of a boatload of settlers that was set on fire by the British army. On a year-round basis, you can see strange lights at sea near the Bathurst coast. For some witnesses, as they got closer to the burning image, the boat disappeared, taking its mysterious origins along with it. Other people have seen the boat up close and some have actually made out people burning on deck. For them, the image stays with them a lifetime, burning a lasting picture in their memories that they cannot easily push aside. Such is the case for Bathurst storyteller, researcher and writer Florence Godin.

Florence first heard about the phantom ship of Baie des Chaleurs when she was a youngster, probably no more than eight or nine years of age. "You know how these things go when you're a child. When you're young like that, you really don't want to hear these things because it scares you so badly. I'll admit that when I heard them, the stories frightened me, and I remember wondering if the stories about the burning ship that appears out of nowhere in the middle of the harbour could be true, but I'd usually tell myself that there's no way they could be. I tried really hard to convince myself of that." It was much easier than accepting that maybe, just maybe, there might be some truth to the legends.

However, Florence quickly adds, all of that changed one night several years ago when, at the age of 14 or 15, she became a true believer in the local legend. Although she isn't sure of the year, she knows it was either 1958 or 1959. "That's been a few years ago, I'll admit that," she laughs. "But I do remember it just like it was yesterday. I will never forgot what I saw that night. It was so vivid and so real. It's something I don't think I'll ever get out of my mind."

The night was cold and dark, Florence remembers, noting that it was winter, January or February. "I was walking across an old span bridge that used to cross from one side of the harbour to the other. It's gone now, but it was a big, old bridge. As I walked across it that night, I noticed something bright out of the corner of my eye. It was like something shimmering, and it was out in the middle of the harbour. I had walked across that bridge many times in the past, and I had never seen anything out there on the water before, so I knew that whatever it was, it wasn't normal. So I just stopped walking, and as I looked out over the water, I became very frightened because I saw a ship out in the middle of the harbour and it was on fire. I mean it was covered in flames, from the top just about all the way down to the water."

At first, Florence assumed the burning ship was one of the local fishing boats that must have broken loose from one of the nearby wharves and floated out into the harbour. How it had caught on fire, she didn't know, but she was convinced someone was in trouble that night. "I didn't know what to do," she admits. "I was in a panic. After all, I was just a kid. I was scared and I got really upset over what I was seeing and thinking about the possibility that someone I knew may have lost their boat. People around here in those days couldn't afford to lose a boat. I knew this could create a great deal of hardship for someone."

Instinctively, Florence turned and ran back toward town to get help. "As I did, I noticed car lights approaching me on the bridge. As the car got closer, I stepped off the curb and into the road hoping to get the driver's attention and praying the car would stop. I got right in the middle of the road and waved my hands to flag him down. I was relieved when the car stopped, and I saw that it was a taxi. Inside, there was the driver, of course, and two passengers, one beside the driver in the front seat and the other in the back."

As Florence related the story of the burning boat out on the harbour, the three occupants exited the taxi to take a look and to try to figure out what this hysterical young girl was going on about. "I went over to the side of the bridge with them and pointed out the ship. As I looked at it with them, it was only then that I realized this was not the type of boat that we usually see around these parts. I could tell it certainly wasn't a fishing boat. It was big, with at least one mast, which was visible from where I stood, and it was all engulfed in flames. That's when it suddenly hit me. I knew that it must be the phantom ship that I had heard so much about over the years as a child. That's when it spooked me. The colours of the flames from the fire were unlike anything else that I had ever seen before. These flames were very bright orange and yellow—the most brilliant colours I had ever seen before or since then. And the whole boat seemed to be ablaze. There were flames everywhere."

Over the years, Florence remained thankful that the taxi driver and passengers showed up on the bridge that night because they were able to confirm everything she saw. "I know some people are skeptical of these things, but all of us saw it. There's no doubt in my mind about what I saw that night."

As Florence and the others stood on the bridge and watched the mysterious burning ship, the vision became even more curious as they began to make out more details about what was happening on board. "I know it sounds like a stretch, but as I watched, I saw two men on the burning deck, and they were sword fighting. I kid you not. They were sword fighting like you'd see in the movies. I could make it out pretty clearly. In fact, things were so clear that I could even see the ropes and canvass blowing the wind, that's how real it was."

In time, she adds, they even witnessed a third man climb up a ladder into the rigging. "Then, all of a sudden, without warning, the mast began to sway, and then it just came down. As it fell, the flames flared out all around it—it was quite a spectacular sight to see. What amazed me even more though, was that after the mast came down, we could clearly see a woman running on the deck. She was wearing a big hooped skirt like they wore a long time ago. As we watched her running on the deck, we could also see two large dogs running beside her. She was moving to the front of the ship, and right behind her was a man who was chasing her. It was all quite amazing. Suddenly, the man reached out, grabbed the woman's hair and hauled her back to him. Then, as if from out of nowhere, another man was suddenly there, and the two men began fighting. It was all mysterious, but amazing to see."

Florence has no idea how long they stood and watched the burning ship that night. "We just stood there, not believing what we were seeing. It was like we were not aware of the time. It was all very strange. I'm sure all our mouths were hanging wide open at what we were seeing."

Finally, as it was getting late and the temperature was very cold, the three people from the taxi got back into the car and left. Florence remained for a while longer because she found it difficult to pull herself away from the sight of the mysterious ship that was still burning quite brightly even after all that time. Finally, she knew she had to leave, but as she walked the full length of the bridge, she was amazed to see the flames still burning. And, she adds, she could still clearly see the figures of people on the deck.

Over the years, Florence has heard many explanations for the phantom ship. There are many theories, but she has her own thoughts as to its origins. "When I think back on what I saw that night, I really believe that what I witnessed was a massacre on board that ship. One theory has it that the ship is connected to the expulsion of the Acadians some 200 years ago. Apparently, one ship loaded with Acadians was lost, and many people believe that is the phantom ship. I don't believe that. That is not what I saw that night. There is also the suggestion that the ship was owned by a rich Englishman and his wife, who were lost coming to the New World, but I don't think that's what I saw either. A third theory goes back to the time of the pirates that used to sail the waters of the North Atlantic, and that is more in keeping with I saw. I believe that ship, wherever it came from, was attacked and boarded by pirates and then set on fire. I think that's what we saw that night."

Many people have seen the phantom ship, and many people believe that seeing it is actually a bad omen, a sign of bad luck or that a terrible storm is approaching. But Florence doesn't buy into that. "I believe what we have here are lost souls trapped on that burning ship, looking for someone to help them. I guess we will never know."

Ghost of the Keyhole Mine

New Brunswick ghost writer David Goss tells an interesting story about the ghost of the Keyhole Mine. He says Charlotte County proved to be the richest source of ghost tales as he collected for a column he wrote for the *Moncton Times & Transcript* from 1999 to 2004. "Most of the tales were fragmentary and I had to do a lot of chasing to pull them together, but occasionally, a story would come that would need no revision or further development." He often tells the tale that follows, which he learned from Daniel Justason of Pennfield, who called it "The Legend of the Keyhole Mine."

In the 1890s, three men followed the shore south from Saint John and discovered a silver deposit in the dense forest of Red Head Harbour. They landed their boat at Doherty's Beach and cut trails inland until they were able to clear a camp site. They named their mine the Keyhole Mine after a giant rock formation carved by the incessant pounding of the Fundy tides. Where these men came from and exactly who they were is lost in time. The only thing left to tell of their existence is a flooded open-pit mine deep in the woods and the ghost of one miner who refused to give up.

At the end of the 19th century, there were few homes along the serpentine dirt road that winds along the rugged shoreline of Seeley's Cove and Red Head. At Red Head, during winter when the ground was frozen and snow lay deep on the trails, the miners boarded at the home of John Lloyd. In spring, summer and fall, they worked hard at their mine and found a fair amount of silver. The sound of the maul hitting the metal hand drill to make the holes for dynamite could be heard echoing across Red Head Harbour. Day and night, these men worked hard until the long hours began to take their toll.

Two of the men, known now only as Bill and Tom, were older and more experienced. The third, Joshua, was younger and knew little about the use of dynamite. From all accounts, these three men worked well together, indulging in only occasional disagreements. That may be the reason that Bill and Tom failed to notice the gradual changes in Joshua. As time passed, he became obsessed with success and didn't want to stop digging even to eat. He became suspicious of his two partners, believing they were trying to cheat him and even kill him for his share. His clothing became ragged and dirty. He stopped washing and shaving and began staying awake at night—Joshua was going mad in his quest for riches.

Gradually, the mine played out. Bill and Tom decided to leave and look elsewhere for silver. Joshua disagreed and a fight started. He accused his partners of trying to cheat him, and vowed he would not leave until he found the silver vein again. He grabbed a gun and told them to leave.

Bill and Tom packed their belongings and left Joshua to work the worthless hole. When they had gone a few miles, a great explosion shook the ground and a large cloud of dust billowed up into the sky. The men returned to the pit but found it full of water and no sign of Joshua. Bill said, "Well, I guess his ghost will be working the mine now." They left, and nothing more is known of them.

In 1908, two men named Matthew Harding and Enos Justason built a weir at Red Head. As they worked on the water, they could hear the sound of a maul beating on a hand drill deep in the woods where the mine had been. This pounding has been heard by subsequent owners of the weir for 100 years.

After several investigations, no clue can be found to explain the source of the strange pounding. It is heard day or night. Locally, people believe it is Joshua's ghost still searching for the silver deposit.

For those who might like to hear the tapping or search for the mine, the Red Head Road is seaward off New Brunswick Route 1 about seven kilometres west of New River Beach.

The Ghost of John

New Brunswick author and folklorist, David Goss, says he really would like to meet a ghost. "With all the stories I've collected and told both orally and in written form, I'm surprised that not one of those restless spirits from the other side hasn't appeared by now to correct some mistake I've made with the material," he says. "Certainly the living are quick to correct errors they see, but perhaps ghosts are kinder than we imagine. Perhaps they don't care about grammatical errors in my text as much as a Saint John teacher who called me regularly to tell me I should know better. Perhaps ghosts don't care about spelling, or punctuation mistakes, so long as I've gotten the facts right. After all, I haven't made up the stories I've recounted on walk 'n' talks and in newspaper and magazine articles. I haven't had to, for as I always say, I cannot say what the truth may be, I only report what was told to me."

And plenty has been told. But when it comes to the ghost story he uses most often, that of the ghost of New River Beach, well, he cannot say that that is the procedure he has followed. So, if any ghost should be upset, it is that of the unknown stevedore from the barque *Genii* who washed up in Deadman's Cove on the Barnaby Head Nature Trail following the Saxby gale of October 4, 1869. "In order to bring this fellow alive—so to speak—I've even given him a name—John Nathanial Leavitt—and when I position myself on the rattle rock beach near the cave in the cove where he is reputed to dwell these days, I greet those passing by with a song, and it goes like this:

"Have you seen the ghost of John,
Long white bones with no skin on.

Oooohhhhhooooouuuuuggggggghhhhhh!
Wouldn't it be chilly with no skin on?

"Now, to that point, the only liberties I've taken are with the name and the song. The ghost has been seen by numerous folk in that cove and along the beach. Some people say they see his crushed body only from waist to feet; others from waist to head. Some claim to have seen him carrying his head under his arm while walking the beach, while still others are certain they have seen his shadowy and ragged countenance in a home overlooking the beach where the other seamen who drowned in the gale were laid out prior to being taken back to Mascarene for burial."

The ghost of Deadman's Cove, though, never got a proper burial, and this is where David takes up the story. "For the past several summers I have been appearing as the ghost in ragged and tattered costume, seaweed strung around my shoulder, old man's beard and dead man's fingers protruding from my toque, blood oozing on my knee bandage, lots of bog dirt rubbed on my legs, arms and face, and heavily dusted with baby powder. The idea is that I look as much as I can like someone who is over 150 years old and has been stumbling along the Fundy coast trying to convince those he meets that he really is the ghost of New River, and if they could find a buckboard and two horses and take him to the Mascarene Cemetery, he could finally lie in peace with the other seamen who died on the barque *Genii*."

So far, though David has appeared across the province from Campobello Island to Moncton, from Saint John to Jacquet River, no one has been able to help. "I am not surprised by this, as I tell the audiences I've been seeking help since 1869.

"I share stories with them of pirates and tell them of a ghost pirate that scared off treasure hunters on Grand

Manan, and I tell them that I, John Nathanial Leavitt, was there, and I saved those treasure hunters from a terrible death.

"I tell them John Nathanial Leavitt is behind the legend of the Ghost of Saint John West, one Daniel Keymore who was swamped and drowned off the Bay Shore, but whose wife never believed him to be dead. A codfish showed up on her doorstep each year on the anniversary of his death. I tell the folks that John Nathanial Leavitt was placing that codfish, and hoping she would see me.

"I share stories of hoping to be seen while walking with prisoners abandoned on a beach at Little Lepreau who still rattle their chains night after night. I tell of a little girl in Dipper Harbour I rescued from a shark attack, then I'm out in a dory with a Grand Manan fisherman who sees a phantom ship on fire and is about to drown when I pull him to safety. But none of them will help old John."

In each session, David says he leaves behind a smattering of New Brunswick history and geography, and shares some Fundy shore traditions and folktales for those who hear the stories to think about. "Each summer as I do the presentations, I hear some new stories, and these often lead to further adventures for John Nathanial Leavitt to share over winter with school classes, at sleepovers or at other special occasions."

Hopefully, he adds, the ghost of New River will not be any more upset with the new stories than he has been with those told over the past few years!

The Dungarvon Whooper

The legend of the Dungarvon Whooper (pronounced "hooper") tells the story of a sinister murder that took place in the late 19th century at a logging camp along the Dungarvon River in central New Brunswick. A small place of few inhabitants, the camp was located about 45 minutes upriver from what today is the city of Miramichi. Supposedly based on actual events that happened a long time ago, the legend has been immortalized for future generations in a song written by Michael Whelan. Ian Ross, a Nova Scotia based researcher and journalist, learned about the Dungarvon Whooper while he worked as a reporter at the city's newspaper, the *Miramichi Leader*. Although he now works and lives in Halifax, he still enjoys the story and likes to share it with others.

According to Ross, the story of the Dungarvon Whooper goes back to a young fellow named Ryan who went to work as a cook at a logging camp in the thick, dense forests that surrounded the young settlements of the Miramichi. With its strategic location along the Miramichi River, its proximity to the ocean and a seemingly endless supply of raw materials from the nearby forests, the Miramichi region became a hub of activity in the lumber industry with many logging operations and mills.

Like hundreds of young men in those days, hardworking Ryan was attracted to the forestry industry by its promise of steady work and good pay. Over time, with few places to spend his money, Ryan accumulated a healthy stash that, according to local legend, he kept with him always, carrying it in a thick, fat money belt that he never let out of his sight. One day, when the work crews returned to the camp from a full day of logging in the woods, they discovered Ryan face down on the ground. He was dead, and his bulging money belt was missing.

The boss—the only other person left behind at the camp with Ryan during the day while the others were out logging—told the men that the young fellow had fallen seriously ill and died unexpectedly from his sudden sickness. The other men knew better and concluded that the older man had murdered Ryan for his money.

Because the camp was located miles away from the nearest settlement and because the early spring thaw had made the roads all but impassible, the men decided to bury Ryan's remains near the camp. They placed his body, which has never been recovered, in a shallow grave near a spring and returned to camp.

Later that same night, as the men were attempting to get some sleep, they heard a loud yelling and whooping sound. The noise was so loud and persistent that it kept the men from falling asleep all that night. Everyone believed it was the spirit of young Ryan returning to the camp to seek vengeance for his untimely death. The next morning, the entire crew was so spooked from the night's events that they packed up everything and left the camp, never to return.

Sometime later, the company, successful in hiring a replacement crew, reopened the camp. However, it wasn't long before the new crew fled the site amid reports of a terrible, ear-shattering whooping sound. Eventually, the lumber company was forced to close down its camp near Dungarvon because, as word spread about the Whooper, it could not attract workers to the site.

The haunting sounds continued for years and were heard by everyone who visited the site of the lumber camp until Father Murdock, a priest from the nearby town of Renous, was asked to put the poor spirit to rest once and for all. Standing over the wilderness grave, Father Murdock read some holy words from the Bible and made a sign of the cross. Some people say Father Murdock succeeded in quieting the ghost, but others insist the fearful cries of Ryan can still be heard to this day, and they fear to visit the grave by Whooper Spring.

The story of the Dungarvon Whooper is the stuff of Maritime legend. A passenger train running from Newcastle to Fredericton along the Miramichi River was named the Dungarvon Whooper because the sound of the train's whistle reminded everyone of the legend. Operating mostly on a railway originally built by New Brunswick businessmen Alexander Gibson and Jabez Bunting Snowball, the train was later part of the Canadian National Railway system. It ceased operation in the early 1960s.

The Ghost of Sculley Beach

Old Man Sculley lived in a rundown house in Douglastown, once a small New Brunswick hamlet but now a suburb of the city of Miramichi. His house, located near St. Mark's Cemetery, was close by the ocean shore at a pleasant, secluded place where many of the locals would often go to enjoy a walk on the beach or to swim on a hot summer day. Old Man Sculley, however, was a cranky and crotchety old gentleman. He was a recluse who, for some unknown reason, had a major dislike of children, especially teenagers. He would often chase them away from his beach waving his cane high in the air and throwing things at them. Whether he would have done them harm if he could have caught them isn't known for sure, but most of the townsfolk avoided the old man.

While teenagers were fearful of the old man, they also taunted him, as teenagers often do to someone of such character. One day, though, when Old Man Sculley failed to show up at the edge of his property to chase off a group of young trespassers, they became worried about him. They knew the old man would not condone them being there, and if he didn't show up to chase them off, there must be a good reason.

As the days went by and Old Man Sculley still did not come out, the teenagers became even more concerned and suspected that something drastic had happened. Finally, one boy became brave enough to venture farther onto the old man's property to investigate. Fearing for his safety and thinking the old man might be lying in wait somewhere along the route, the teenager gingerly made his way to one of the dirty windows and, peering through the grime and salty buildup, looked inside. As his eyes adjusted to the darkness of the home's dingy interior, the boy was startled to see the man's limp, lifeless body hanging from the rafters—Old Man Sculley had killed himself.

Now, on certain nights when the conditions are just right, the ghost of Old Man Sculley can be seen walking the shores of the beach he loved so much and looking for trespassers, especially teenagers, to chase off. Believe it or not.

*　　*　　*

In the Maritimes

• It is considered bad luck for a pregnant woman to cross her legs.

• If the bottom of your feet itch, it means somebody has been walking over the ground that will someday be your grave.

More Miramichi Mysteries

Wendy Patterson, the assistant editor of the weekly newspaper the *Miramichi Leader,* heard this story many years ago and still finds it fascinating.

There is a house in Loggieville, a small northern New Brunswick settlement near Chatham, that was built well over 100 years ago by a fisherman. The locals claim the place is haunted by the spirit of an infant. Although there is no record of a death in the home, one can assume that because of its age, not all of its history is known.

"Regardless, they say that it is possible, on occasion, to hear a child crying in the house, and it seems to be coming from the walls," Wendy says. "According to one of the stories, a woman who once lived there had a baby, and she invited a friend to come and stay with her. The next day, when the woman asked her friend how she had slept, the friend replied that she had had a terrible sleep because the baby had kept her awake all night. The homeowner was shocked. Turning to her friend, she said that was simply not possible because her baby had slept soundly through the entire night. Apparently, this type of thing happened a lot."

Wendy says there are more ghost stories from the area. Some people believe the Wilson's Point train bridge is haunted. "They say a guy who was intoxicated many years back wandered out onto the bridge and into the path of an oncoming train. He was killed instantly. Nowadays, he is supposedly seen walking the train bridge."

Then there is the story of the wizard of the Miramichi as told by Ian Ross, another Maritime journalist who has researched local ghost stories. He says that according to legend, "this young lad was working with his older brother out in the fields when strange things started to happen. It seems the younger brother could get his work done within the bat of an eyelash, and no one could understand how. The locals insisted he must be using magic. How else could they explain the strange happenings?"

When the young fellow was finally charged with using magic, he disappeared, but not before the townsfolk noticed that when he walked, he left behind hoof prints.

And there's the story Ian tells of a young woman who insists she sees her grandfather, even though he's been dead for many years. "She says she has seen her grandfather through the window of his house, and the rocking chair that he would sit in will start moving on its own power. Next to the chair, purple stains appear on the floor. That's where the old man would sit and eat grapes."

As with all ghost stories, these have become part of a larger mosaic, a collection of tales and legends that make up the community's personality. They can't be explained, and the question must be asked, why should they be?

The Ghost-Guarded Treasure

Legend suggests that Prince Edward Island is a mother lode for buried treasure, and that means there are many stories of ghosts. Allan MacRae, who has been writing a column for the *West Prince Graphic* for 25 years called "From Our Past," collects stories of Prince Edward Island history and genealogy. He shares a story he found from a column titled "Legends of PEI" by Uncle Joe that appeared in the December 3, 1948 issue of *The Charlottetown Guardian*. One of his favourite ghost stories from the island is a tale of buried treasure and its ghostly gaurds.

Somewhere near Georgetown, Prince Edward Island, lies buried treasure of gold coins. Legend suggests that between the districts of Lorne Valley and Riverton lies hidden a fortune that would make its finders rich beyond their wildest dreams. The story has been passed down from the days of the French Regime, and a strange tale it is.

On a bleak, stormy night many years ago, a pirate ship laden with treasure put into Georgetown Harbour. Its occupants went ashore, buried their plunder and then put out to sea. They were being chased by a French warship, and, not wishing to lose so valuable a cargo should they be captured, the treasure was hastily buried close to the harbour until such time as it could be safely removed to a better hideout. That the yellow metal carried the curse of the buccaneers who had plundered ships and killed men for its taking, goes without saying. The gold, 12 iron pots of it, was discovered by a party of Acadians, taken at night and carried to its present place of concealment. They were later deported to France and never lived to return to the New World.

After the disgraceful act of deportation had been carried out, the British took over the occupation of St. John's Island, now Prince Edward Island. Emigrants from the British Isles began arriving on the shores of the island to carve homes from the wilderness in this corner of the New World. Gradually, the land was cleared and brought under cultivation, and little hamlets, as well as isolated dwellings, sprang up here and there. But the forests that covered the districts of Lorne Valley and Riverton were among the last to fall to the axes of settlers. The Lorne Valley district was settled by a small band of Scottish people who emigrated from the Isle of Skye over 200 years ago. And it was one person of this group who came across the pirates' gold while hunting down a bear that had killed two of his sheep.

While crawling on hands and knees through a jungle of underbrush, his hands came in contact with an iron handle. When he tried to pry it loose, he found it attached to a small iron pot. Using the point of his musket for a crowbar, he finally succeeded in dragging the thing from its hiding place. Other similar vessels lay buried beneath the one he had unearthed. How many there were he could not tell, for by this time he had made a further discovery that sent his blood coursing through his veins like a springtime freshet.

The iron pot that lay before his eyes was filled to the very brim with gold coins. And so were the second and third ones. Now almost beside himself with excitement as he gazed upon the sea of coins and watched them falling through his fingers, he pondered the sudden wealth the fates had unceremoniously thrust into his lap.

But his thoughts were cut short by the sudden feeling of a bony hand on his shoulder and the sound of a strange voice crying out loudly, "Avast thar, ye thievin' son o' a landlubber. If it weren't fer this peg leg o' mine, I'd cut the tongue from yer rotten carcass, so I would. Avast thar! And let the gold that me and me chums took from the bones of dead men—and livin' ones too—lie where it be."

The terrified settler looked up to see a group of ghosts standing beside him. They were a bloodthirsty lot, if appearances counted for anything. Their faces showed the scars of battle, and two of them had empty sleeves where once their arms had been. And one, who appeared to be their leader, strutted about on a peg leg, cursing and swearing in a manner dreadful to hear. The man tried to speak, but the tongue in his mouth was frozen. He tried to run, but his legs had lost their power to move.

"Coward!" cried the spook with the peg leg. "I niver knowed a landlubber yet that had guts enough to talk back to a buccaneer. Let's strip him and teach him not go nosing into other folks' property."

While two ghosts were busy tearing off the man's clothing, a third fellow stepped forward and, drawing his sword, brought the flat of the blade down on the prisoner's back with such force as to cause him cry out in agony.

"Give him a bit more of that medicine," another ghostly spectre hissed. Several more strokes were laid on the poor man's naked back, but this time he held his peace.

"Now, turn him loose, mates, and may the devil swallow him, boots and all, if he ever comes a-snoopin round this place of ours again."

Battered and beaten, the settler finally reached home completely exhausted, and no wonder; the poor chap had had a terrible experience. Questions were put to him thick and fast. The folks of the district naturally wanted to learn what had happened while he had been off on his bear-chasing expedition. But this man gave no information. His tongue was sealed by fear of what the spooks might do to him should he talk too much.

From then on, the fellow grew more silent and withdrew himself from all company. They say he lived only about six months after his great ordeal, and when he lay on his death-bed, he summoned a few of his trusted neighbours and told them the story you have just read.

The secret was too big to keep. The yarn soon got nosed about, and people from far and near rushed like madmen to seek the treasure. Ghosts or devils—it was all the same to the hungry, grasping adventurers who took up the hunt. Come hell or high water, they would find the gold and wrest it from its hiding place.

The woods around Riverton and Lorne Valley were torn from their roots. They soil was dug into, levelled and redug time and again, but all was in vain. One by one, the searchers gave up and returned to their fields and tended to their flocks. Some maintained the story was nothing but a myth; others claimed they had discovered the exact spot where the gold had lain, but that the ghosts had removed it to a new hiding place that may never be discovered. If it still lies buried where the band of French Acadians are supposed to have hidden it, no living mortal can tell. Today, the tale must be looked upon as just another legend—the legend of the ghost-guarded treasure.

The Legend of the Tolling Bell

On the morning of October 7, 1858, the city of Charlottetown, Prince Edward Island, was all agog over a strange happening that has not been solved to this day. People who believed in the supernatural called it a first-rate ghost story, but others claimed it was only a myth. Journalist Allan MacRae, in the *West Prince Graphic,* writes, "Here's the yarn as was heard from the lips of old-timers in the 1940s, cemented together by a few bits of historical data taken from an old Island newspaper of 1858. The yarn is the Legend of the Tolling Bell."

Captain Cross awoke early and, according to a custom of his, set out to take a ride in Victoria Park before having his breakfast. In order to procure his saddle pony, which was housed at the Royal Oak Stables, he set out on foot and was just about to cross Black Sam's bridge when the sound of a tolling bell broke the silence of that early October morning. Believing that the sound came from some foreign ship in the harbour, he proceeded down Pownal Street until he came within full view of the waterfront. But there were no large ships to be seen. A few small fishing craft were moored to the wharf or rode at anchor a short distance out. That was all.

The captain then turned about and had started to retrace his steps up Pownal Street when the sound of the bell reached his ears for the second time. Now he knew he had been mistaken in thinking the sound came from the harbour. It was a church bell, and he was sure it was coming from the old kirk. He quickened his pace and, for the time being, forgot all about the Royal Oak Stables and his morning ride.

Once more, the bell rang out loud and clear. Cross stopped and counted. One, two, three—three times it tolled. This time there could be no mistake. It was the bell in the belfry of St. James Church. But why would it be tolling at such an hour? Surely nobody was being buried so early in the morning. Cross was puzzled and full of curiosity. The whole thing seemed ridiculous and a bit uncanny.

Captain Cross quickened his pace. Not a living soul was to be seen on the streets, but being a man of considerable courage, he ventured on alone. When he came within view of the church, his startled gaze fell upon three white-clad figures standing beside the open door. As his gaze swept across the eerie scene, he noted that the creatures were barefooted and without any kind of head covering. For the space of a moment, Captain Cross stood still in his tracks. It was not a sight to inspire confidence, and many a person of lesser courage would have turned and fled.

He took a few steps forward and addressed the strange company, but they did not seem to hear his words or notice his presence. Then the door closed.

From somewhere nearby came the sound of running feet. The captain looked around and saw the church sexton draw up beside him, breathless and full of excited curiosity. The captain whispered a few words in the sexton's ear and the latter began to shake like one afflicted with the ague. The captain looked at him reprovingly and said, "Come!"

The two men ascended the steps of the church together and tried the door. It was locked. The windows were fastened, too. As they tried the last one, they saw the ghostlike figure of a woman ascending the stairs leading to the belfry. The sexton grew white as death and turned about as if to run away when Cross laid a heavy hand on his shoulder and commanded in a stern voice, "Cut the nonsense, sexton, and go fetch the keys."

"The very flesh has left my bones," said the sexton as he started off for the keys. When he arrived back a few minutes later, he was accompanied by the minister, who appeared anxious but excited.

When Captain Cross had found the right key and opened the door, the three men stepped across its threshold. "I'm going upstairs to investigate that belfry," said the captain. "Who will follow me?"

"I won't," said the sexton. "I've seen enough already, and besides, it's dangerous to get mixed up with spirits."

"Coming, parson?" asked Captain Cross as he started up.

"Well…maybe I'd better stay here and keep the sexton company," he replied.

The captain threw a withering glance at the two of them and continued to climb. Then the bell tolled six times. The captain went on. The sexton and the minister withdrew to the church grounds, just in case. Before the captain reached the belfry, the bell tolled once more, but the captain vowed he would see the end of the drama, come what may.

Finally, the last step was taken; the trap door leading to the tower was flung up; but there was nothing to be seen save the old kirk bell resting amid dust and spider webs.

History tells us that on Friday, the seventh day of October, 1858, the steamer *Fairy Queen* foundered off the coast of Pictou, Nova Scotia, carrying to death seven people, three of whom were members of the old kirk.

4
Less Ghostly (But Still Mysterious) Local Legends

The Energy Field of Oak Island

To do a collection of Maritime ghost stories and legends and leave out the world-famous Oak Island, located just off the rugged, yet picturesque, south coast of Nova Scotia, is almost a crime. We've visited this mysterious place before (see *Ghost Stories of the Maritimes, Vol. 1*). In comparison to Oak Island, other legends from this part of Canada are but pale imitations, so it's time to return to this mysterious place that has attracted treasure seekers and ghost hunters from around the world for centuries.

The mystique and aura that surround Oak Island date back to 1795, when the hunt for an elusive treasure began. Theories abound as to what is buried beneath the rocky, coarse soil of this small island that has spawned dozens of books and countless ghost stories. Many men have lost fortunes and their lives trying to solve the clues, hoping to ultimately unlock the treasure vault, but to date, the island has refused to give up its secret. Over the past 200 years, many theories have been put forward about the treasure. Perhaps the most popular of those theories is that it is a rich booty buried there by a band of bloodthirsty pirates, most notably Captain Kidd, who plied the waters of the Atlantic Ocean hundreds of years ago. Other theories suggest the stash is ancient Inca treasure or that it is the lost manuscripts of William Shakespeare. Some even theorize that the treasure is the Arc of the Covenant, hidden there by the Knights Templar, who were known to have visited the New World long before other early European explorers. The theories are as limited as one's imagination.

This monument is dedicated to the memory of those who lost their lives while trying to unlock the centuries-old secrets of Oak Island off Nova Scotia's southern shore.

Although now privately owned and off limits, Oak Island was at one time open to the public. Years ago, well-received walking tours were being offered by the Nova Scotia Department of Tourism together with treasure-hunting syndicate Triton Alliance Corporation. Many guides were hired to meet the wide-eyed public and direct them around the various shafts, holes, trenches and pits that bore witness to the sometimes frantic search that has taken as many as six lives.

A local group is currently trying to convince the government of Nova Scotia to purchase Oak Island and return it to the public domain so that treasure hunters and mystery lovers can once again explore its natural wonders. One of the driving forces behind this effort is amateur historian Danny Hennigar. He recalls working on the island as a guide and notes that he and his young colleagues were merely high school and university students. He fondly recalls the experience. "Once we donned our mandatory pirate head scarf, sash, black pants, striped shirt and name tag, we became animated interpreters, a term so foreign to us and yet, for the time, so cutting edge too. Men, women, boys and girls. We all learned the art of meeting the public and giving them the best Oak Island experience we could muster," he says.

Daily, rain or shine, tourists from all over the world traversed the 185-metre-long, one-lane causeway that links Oak Island with the mainland. They came by the hundreds to take the island tour. Some were looking for activities to wear out high-strung youngsters cooped up in hot cars all day; others had read about the island's fascinating history in one of the hundreds of juicy magazine or newspaper articles written about the little island. Still others were students of the story bent on solving the mystery of Oak Island.

Danny explains that tour guides were stationed at various points along the route to direct tourists and keep them from getting lost, answer questions and give presentations on special points of interest. The positions were rotated so the guides were able to learn all aspects of the entire island, and by the end of the summer, they were all experts.

"One of the least exciting spots to be stationed all day was called the Ox Pen, where a local man kept a beautiful pair of brown and white oxen who grazed lazily all day long in a fenced off field," Danny recalls. "The animals were aloof, often staying at the back part of the pen, but on occasion, they would amble up to the front and give a lucky tourist an impressive glimpse of the Nova Scotia quintessential 'work horse.' We were expected to answer questions about the oxen, but one of our primary goals was to keep people off private property owned by a rival treasure hunter who had long been embroiled in a land dispute with Triton Alliance." He says that because the road to the Money Pit forked at the Ox Pen, it was essential that visitors were directed to follow the road to the right that deposited them onto what became known as the beach road, thus avoiding the other treasure hunter's land. Tourists were then expected to follow the beach road back to the parking lot.

"On one particularly lonely, slow day," Danny remembers, "I was stationed at the Ox Pen along with a fellow guide. Relaxing on one of the many picnic tables positioned strategically here and there, we passed the time by talking about our limited life experiences, girls, parties, school and, of course, Oak Island gossip. It was easy to keep track of the few tourists who passed by us on their way to the Money Pit and all the other attractions. It was late in the afternoon, and most of the visitors had returned, heading back to their cars in the parking lot. It was a hot day, even though the fog hung off the outer islands."

At that point, he says, they saw a lone man running and walking very quickly up the beach road, looking back over his shoulder like the devil himself was giving chase. "His eyes were as big as saucers, and he was breathless when he reached our position. We thought perhaps he had lost his party or had been spooked by one of the ever-present grouse that inhabited the island. Between breaths he related his story to us."

According to Danny, this fellow said he had been walking along the beach, leisurely taking in the beauty and cool breeze that flowed off the restless Atlantic. He entered the close confines of the beach road, bordered on the right by the larger of the island's two swamps, and on the left by a close, thick growth of spruce trees, alder bushes and pines. "As he walked, he passed from an area of cool air immediately into a wall of hot air. He said he could easily stand with half of his body in hot air and the other half in cold air. He said he stepped into it, then out of it, back and forth. He said the trees seemed to close in on him, and he was suddenly seized with fear and trepidation to the point that the hairs rose on his neck, and he had a horrible feeling of foreboding and gut-tural fear. He seemed like a lucid person to me, but he was awash with sweat by the time he reached us, and he was in no mood to go back down to experience the odd phenome-non with two guides as witnesses this time. Babbling about energy fields, spirits and his eerie encounter, in no time flat, he had hustled down the centre road, never looking back, and headed straight for his car."

The people who worked at the reception centre later told Danny that this man went directly to his vehicle, jumped in his car and sped off the island in a cloud of dust. He was spooked, they said. There was little doubt about that.

"With our imaginations piqued, my fellow guide and I walked down the road to the beach and experienced no such conditions. All seemed normal to us, if not a little extra peaceful and quiet. Later, I passed the incident off as a possible temperature inversion, or the cool air of the swamp and nearby ocean mixing with the warmth of the woods. I am a pragmatic person, not given to believe in the supernatural or ghosts, but I do have an open mind. That man was frightened, you could read it in his eyes. I know adult men who would not consider spending a night on Oak Island. I have heard ghost stories of red-eyed dogs, mysterious crows and spirits in the form of long-dead soldiers who march the island's pathways, but have never seen anything myself."

They say that the eyes are the windows to the soul. Many years later, as a police officer, Danny says he has seen that fear in people's eyes time and again after near-death experiences, car accidents or even a simple brush with the law. "I always come back to recall that day on Oak Island and the man on the beach road. There is no doubt that man was scared."

Did this tourist encounter one of the ghosts that are said to roam the famous Oak Island, or can his experience be explained as an unusual atmospheric phenomenon? Let's just chalk it up as another experience that defies explanation.

The Bloody Handprint of
Covey Island

On May 8, 1756, on a 108-acre, nondescript island strategically stationed in what is today known as Mahone Bay, Louis Payzant was murdered and scalped, but not before leaving his mark on the landscape of Nova Scotian folklore. At the same time, a 12-year-old boy, a servant and her infant also met their untimely fates on Covey Island, once known as Payzant Island. But the brutal and bloody deaths of these early settlers is only part of the story.

This 108-acre island in Mahone Bay is the location for a local legend known as the Bloody Handprint of Covey Island.

To better understand the mystery of Covey Island and the place it holds in Canadian history, we turn to Ontario-based researcher and author Linda Layton. The legend that surrounds the killings on the island is best known locally for the bloody handprint that is emblazoned on a rock that sits a fair distance from where it is believed the Payzant homestead was located more than 250 years ago, and Linda says that is what ultimately led her to the legend of Covey Island.

The author, who works as a library cataloguer, first heard the incredible story many years ago. "I became interested in genealogy and the story when I was in my teens," Linda says. But her fascination with the history soon became much more, particularly following her grandmother's death in 1961. While cleaning out the older woman's personal belongings, she discovered a newspaper clipping that recounted the story of the bloody handprint on the rock at Covey Island. From there, she was driven to find out more about the fascinating story that was part of her family's history. "It just worked its way up from an interest, to a hobby, to an obsession," she recalls. "I just wanted to find everything I could about my family."

Linda's search to find "everything" meant wading through many stories containing embellished information. As she puts it, "Over the years, this story has been handed down to different generations orally, and it has been enhanced and altered." However, her extensive search also led her to some delightful surprises. Topping the list of highlights was a pair of visits to Covey Island, where she explored an old house foundation and the famed bloody handprint.

But Linda, who highly treasures the truth, doesn't buy the folklore explanation for the imprint on the rock. She believes the scientific explanation for the markings, which suggests that iron deposits have rusted in the rock. Still, she concedes that there is a side of her that understands why the folklore story is much more fascinating. "It is wonderful to keep the story alive," she says. "It's far more interesting than just iron deposits on a rock."

The story of the bloody handprint begins with her great-great-great-great-grandmother, Marie Anne Payzant. Marie Anne's epic journey began when, as a Huguenot, she fled from France to Jersey to escape religious persecution. In Jersey, Marie Anne met and married Louis Payzant, who had also fled to Jersey to escape Catholicism. In 1753, the couple and their four children left a comfortable life on the island of Jersey and sailed across the Atlantic to settle in Lunenburg and, in 1755, built a home on Payzant Island, now Covey Island, in Mahone Bay.

Within a year, a Maliseet raiding party, which was loyal to the French, landed on the island, killed and scalped Louis (and the three others previously mentioned), took a pregnant Marie Anne and her children captive and burned their cabin. It is said that in the last few minutes of his life, Louis grabbed his bleeding chest, and in one last act of desperation, fell back onto a rock beside the front door, bracing himself with his bloody hand. The intense heat from the burning cabin seared the handprint into the boulder, where it can still be seen today. The rock has since been moved down the hill, where it sits near the beach. Early in the last century, one local entrepreneur built a small structure over the rock and charged a nominal fee to anyone who wanted to see the famed handprint.

As for Marie Anne and the Payzant children, the Maliseet raiders took the family through Acadia to Quebec by canoe. Marie Anne was kept as a prisoner of war for four years, and the children were adopted by the Maliseet tribe and the Jesuits. Marie Anne and her children survived the ordeal and

The mystery that surrounds the "handprint" seen on this rock on Covey Island is the stuff of local legend.

The Mystery of Jerome

Although the mysterious story of Jerome isn't exactly a ghost story in the traditional sense, its unusual place in the annals of Nova Scotian history and folklore has earned it the right to be included in this collection of the unexplained. As you read on, you'll see why.

In the early morning hours of a fine September day in 1863, near Digby, Nova Scotia, a fisherman busily gathered rock weed along the shore in a place called Sandy Cove on the Bay of Fundy. It wasn't long before he noticed a dark figure nestled alongside a big rock on the beach. At first, he thought it was a seal because they are common in the area. However, as the fisherman got closer, he saw that the figure was that of a huddled man, his legs wrapped in bloodied cloth. Upon inspection, he found that both of the man's legs had been amputated just above the knees. It appeared that the mystery man's legs had been amputated by a skilled surgeon, but the stumps were only partially healed and bandaged. The man was also suffering from cold and exposure.

Beside the man in the sand was a jug of water and a tin of biscuits. There were footprints on the beach, and blowing about were a few strips of linen that could have been bandages. The only clue as to the man's identity was that when he moaned and tried to speak, it was in a foreign language that the fisherman did not understand. The fisherman later recalled he had seen a ship passing back and forth the day before, about a kilometre offshore in St. Mary's Bay. Residents of the area concluded the man must have been brought in from the ship after dark and left on shore.

The castaway, who was about 25 years of age, was carried to the home of Mr. Gidney in nearby Mink Cove, where he was wrapped in warm blankets and given hot drinks. Through the moaning and muttering, only one word was understood. Witnesses said they heard him whisper, "Jerome." So, thinking that might be his name, that is what local residents took to calling the stranger in their midst.

Following a physical examination, it was discovered that Jerome's hands were not calloused, which implied he was not of the working class. As well, the stranger's clothing was curious. His waistcoat was delicately lined and was unmistakably of a foreign pattern. His shirt was of the finest linen, while his knee-length pants were made of a material unknown to the people of Digby. Speculation up and down the bay soon led many to believe he had attempted a mutiny and was punished by amputation. Others suggested the mysterious man had been tossed from a pirate ship, perhaps as a punishment for some unspeakable deed. Most thought, however, that he was heir to a fortune and had been crippled and cast away to make way for someone else seeking his inheritance. None of the stories has ever been proven.

Although Jerome was almost terrified of most adults, he seemed fond of children. He spent most of his time with children and seemed to enjoy watching them play. Fitting into the community, Jerome conducted himself with dignity, and when offered money, he would appear humiliated, as if too proud to take a handout. However, he would accept gifts of candy, tobacco and fruit. He was wary of strangers, but in appearance and manner, he was a gentleman and easy to care for. Eventually, he got so that he could move nimbly on his stumps, but he still sat most of the time.

It was clear that Jerome was there to stay. To help cover his expenses, the provincial government contributed two dollars per week toward his keep. Throughout the years, sailors from many countries around the world were brought to Jerome to see if he would speak their language. He still did not speak, but some observers believed that he was familiar with European languages. He would become very angry when any such visitor mentioned Trieste, a city in northeast Italy. Some people believed that he was of noble stature and that he once must have been an officer. From his looks and complexion, they felt he must be French or Italian. In time, Jerome was taken to the home of John Nicholas in Meteghan, who spoke several European languages. Mr. Nicholas tried to break Jerome's silence but failed. Jerome spent seven years with Mr. Nicholas and the remaining 42 years of his life with Deider Comeau and his family at Alphonse de Clare.

As the years went by, Jerome would make his way down to the water's edge on fine days. There he would sit for hours, gazing toward the sea as if he were expecting visitors from beyond the horizon. The locals became and remained convinced that the legless man lived in constant fear of someone or something.

In time, residents noted that Jerome would often spend days in his room gazing from his window toward the sea. Other times he would sit on the floor, his head bowed and his hands folded. About the last 30 years of his life were spent in absolute silence. His eyes held a tortured look, as if some terrible burden rested on his soul. On one occasion, as if in payment for some evil done in the remote past, he pressed his hands against a hot stove. His hands were horribly blistered, but Jerome did nothing to acknowledge the pain.

Many attempts were made to find an identity for this mystery man, but none succeeded. When Jerome died on April 19, 1912, he took with him the secret of his mutilation and of his mysterious arrival on the Bay of Fundy shore. Who was Jerome? Where had he came from? What macabre circumstances had led to his mutilation and abandonment? Those who knew him best believed Jerome had carried within his heart a secret too terrible to divulge. And if silence had been his pledge, he had kept it well. For almost 50 long and monotonous years he had waited for death, and when it came, it found a silent and inscrutable Jerome. A large stone marker bearing the only name "Jerome" can be found in the Meteghan parish cemetery where he was buried.

In summer 2006, Jerome's story made headlines once again when it was declared that the mystery of how the legless, mute man came to the Nova Scotia shore in 1863 may have been solved. Historian John Lutz of the University of Victoria said in August that new information, found in a New Brunswick archive, could hold the key to the mystery. It told of a man who was "exhibiting strange behaviour and couldn't speak. Members of his community rid themselves of the eccentric by tossing him into the sea, but not before surgically amputating his legs." They then set him adrift, hoping he would eventually make it to New England. John Lutz believes this is the same man who ended up in the remote Nova Scotian village near Digby.

Has the mystery of Jerome been finally solved? Not likely, say many of the locals. Not likely.

What Lies Beneath?

There has been many a sailor who has told stories of seeing strange creatures while on the high seas. Their tales of giant creatures with deadly tentacles are the stuff of legends. But are these just the ramblings of men with overheated imaginations, or are they actual eye-witness accounts of creatures yet unknown to science?

In early summer 2003, a Cape Breton fisherman and a helper were headed out to sea to check lobster traps when they saw what they thought was a huge log in the water. According to descriptions later published by various media and several internet websites, the "log" had a head similar to a sea turtle with a brown, snakelike body. They said it was approximately eight metres long and was brown with smooth skin. The creature submerged and surfaced again two minutes later, then repeated this activity many times. The two men observed the creature for about 45 minutes. The fisherman, who had been at sea for over 30 years, later reported that what he had seen was unlike anything he had ever encountered before. Exactly what the pair saw remains a mystery to this day.

Andrew Hebda, curator of zoology at Halifax's Natural History Museum, believes that what this Cape Breton fisherman observed may have been an oarfish. Oarfish are nature's longest fish and have been known to reach up to 18 metres in length. Although the oarfish is normally found in the waters north of Great Britain, he said this particular specimen probably followed a frigid ocean current to the waters off Cape Breton, where it was spotted.

Andrew adds that although this most recent sighting might be explained through scientific knowledge, that is not necessarily the case for all reports. In fact, reported sightings of sea monsters or unidentified sea creatures from around the Maritime provinces and other parts of Atlantic Canada have been recorded for centuries. For example, Crescent Lake, located 400 kilometres west of St. John's, Newfoundland, appears to have its own version of the Loch Ness Monster. Sightings of "Cressie," as it is called by the locals, have taken place several times over the last 50 years. When no Cressie sightings were reported in 2002, residents wondered if perhaps the animal had died. But Cressie, described by witnesses as a "snake-like creature with a fish-like head," resurfaced in summer 2003, thus continuing the legend. And that's precisely how many of these stories are perpetuated.

There have been many reports of strange creatures in Maritime waters dating from the early settlers. On August 6, 1848, on board the *Daedalus* in the Atlantic Ocean, seven men, including the captain, reported seeing a creature that was about 60 feet (18 metres) long and 15 inches (38 centimetres) in diameter. A mane of a soft-looking material flowed down its back. The creature's body was dark brown, and its throat area was yellowish white. According to the witnesses, the creature was swimming approximately 15 miles (25 kilometres) per hour with its head constantly above the water. In modern times, a creature matching this description has been seen off the coast of California by many reputable witnesses, but no one has been able to identify what it is. Although many of these "sea serpent" descriptions are similar to creatures that are thought to be extinct, many other sea monster sights defy explanation.

Andrew says that when we consider that the vast majority of the oceans and seas are unexplored, such reports are natural. It really isn't hard to believe that there are creatures that live so far down or in such remote areas that they are rarely, if ever, seen by humans. The waters of this planet go mostly unexplored. The giant squid, for example, used to be thought of as a creature of myth and legend, but people have found corpses of just such a creature as recently as July 2007. Every year, unknown animals or animals that were thought extinct are miraculously discovered.

It is from those inexplicable sightings that local legends emerge. Andrew says that one of his favourite sea monster stories comes from the River Denny area of Cape Breton. It started with Nicola Denny, a 17th-century businessman who, together with his brother, settled in Nova Scotia and set up several business operations. In total, they launched more than 20 enterprises, many of which failed miserably. However, Nicola Denny became renowned for his meticulous attention to detail. He recorded everything about his ventures and about the province from that time. In one of those written recordings, the early entrepreneur made note of what is believed to be the first sighting of, not a mermaid, but a merman in Canso Harbour in 1656.

The uncanny aspect of this story, Andrew explains, is that it matches beautifully a 1920s letter from a sea captain who used to make the regular Boston to Yarmouth run. In the letter, the captain told his daughter he had seen a mermaid near the Shelburne Bank, which is located off the southern tip of Nova Scotia. "So now we have a reported sighting of a merman and a mermaid," Andrew says. "Is this a coincidence?" He doesn't know, but together, the reports make a fun and intriguing piece of Nova Scotian folklore.

"Reported sightings of unusual sea creatures litter Nova Scotia history," Andrew points out. "There was a sighting in a place called Green Bay, near Lockeport on the province's south shore, in August 1855. A Mr. Cousins reported seeing a sea serpent that followed the fleet for two days, and his description of it is breathtaking. 'A hideous length of undulating terror,' he wrote. It's a beautiful description. They don't write like that anymore."

Mr. Cousins continued, "Its hump was a crest crown with a waving mass of long pendulum hair like a vein—and behind for 40 or 50 feet, were rolling spirals of an immense body. Its head—six or seven feet in length—and it had large saucer-shaped eyes."

It is unclear what Mr. Cousins was talking about in his writings, but Andrew says, "In fact, there are fish that are not too dissimilar to that, but we can't say that's what it was. We do know that things like oarfish can grow up to 60 feet [18 metres] in length. They also have a modified fin on the front that actually looks like a main of hair."

It may be safe to assume that since creatures are discovered or rediscovered all the time, these sea serpents and lake monsters are just waiting their turn to be identified properly…or maybe not.

The Privateers Have Ears

The late 18th century was an interesting time in the coastal waters off Nova Scotia. The American Revolutionary War had made Nova Scotia's shores a sea-based battleground, with parties both loyal to and rebelling against the British Empire cruising the waters in search of glory and plunder. Liverpool, a small hamlet growing up along the picturesque shores of the gently flowing Mersey River, was, by no exaggeration, very much at the centre of the adventures, good and bad. But while some men were out manning vessels, travelling the North Atlantic in search of riches, local merchant John Mullins was content to stay at home and live off the supplementary spoils of war. Nova Scotia based researcher, historian and writer Patrick Hirtle shares this story of greed that became ingrained in the myth of the small community.

A trader of sorts, John Mullins was recruited for the occasional oceangoing adventure, but, by and large, he much preferred making a life for himself and his wife by acquiring goods on land at a bargain basement price—free, if possible—which he would then polish up and trade for more valuable items. Over the years, it was an activity that Mullins had gotten rather good at, and he made the most of the privateering days of the late 18th century. Of course, the Liverpool trader was always careful to make sure he made a reasonable deal, especially with those associates who were known for having one too many ales. Mullins made sure to have witnesses for all his exchanges, and, while he always got the best of a switch, he was very careful to make sure he traded value for value, lest he be accused of cheating a local.

Such an accusation would have resulted in the only punishment fit for a thief in those days: one of the perpetrator's ears would be cut off to compensate the victim of the poor deal.

One evening, after a night's trading endeavours, Mullins was making his way home to his humble little shack along the shoreline, beyond the confines of Liverpool's centre. As he went, he thought he could hear the muffled voices of men and clanging metal in the distance. Curiosity got the best of him, and Mullins honed in on the noises. Careful to conceal himself behind some bushes, he peered down from the cart path he walked upon to the shoreline below. From his perch, he could make out a number of men on the beach, a freshly dug pit and a number of unidentified objects lying nearby on the sand at the base of a large, well-rooted tree. In the glow of the moonlight, the metallic edges of the unusual objects glinted, and Mullins gasped as he realized that he was looking at a number of sea chests. For a few moments, Mullins' mind raced with thoughts of wealth beyond his dreams. He had happened upon the mother of all opportunities—pirates, privateers, whoever they were on the beach below, were unloading their booty on this shore near his home, and once they departed, Mullins would be free to excavate the treasure for himself.

Stifling his excitement, Mullins watched the activity more intently. Much to his chagrin, after a few minutes, he came to the realization that the unidentified men on the beach were not burying the chests, but rather, they were removing them. Dismayed by this development, Mullins gathered his thoughts for a moment and decided that, rather than abandon this rarest of chances, he should lay in wait in the shadows until the marauders had left the area. Then he could sneak down to the shore and search the hole, just in case some valuable nugget had been left behind in the cache. After what seemed like an eternity, the group of men left the pit and moved toward the shore. A few moments more passed, and then the gentle, swishing sound of oars cutting through calm waters arose from below.

Mullins immediately knew that this was his chance: the oars betrayed the presence of a boat in the coastal waters, meaning that the mysterious guests were most certainly under way, likely returning to their primary vessel tucked safely somewhere out of sight in a neighbouring cove. Leaving the safety of his outpost behind, Mullins tiptoed down to the beach and the promising pit, which had not been filled in. Prodding at the sand and seeing a box edge emerge from the dunes, it quickly became clear that there was, indeed, an item of interest left behind. Mullins grabbed a corner and, to his amazement, pulled to the surface a small, copper-framed chest. He beamed at the discovery and was so taken with the development that he failed to notice the approaching steps of some more strangers.

Suddenly realizing he was not alone, he lifted his head only to find the blade of a cutlass staring him in the face. One of the men, stepping forward, asked the trader how he had come to find this secret hiding place. Mullins, fearing what his fate might be, sputtered out a few words, vainly attempting to explain that he had overheard the commotion from the road on his way home.

"Well," the shadowy figure responded, "a fine pair of ears ye have, m'friend. And since y'likes digging, I have a job for ye. Don't worry," the stranger added in a sinister way, "ye shall be paid for your work."

At morning's light, farther down the beach, Hannah Mullins awoke to find that her husband was nowhere to be found. Alarmed that her little night owl had failed to come home the night before, Mrs. Mullins went into Liverpool to track him down. Unable to find anyone who had seen her John, she begged for help from the townsfolk. They somewhat grudgingly conceded to organize a search party to find the missing man.

A thorough examination of the countryside eventually led the party to the secluded beach where Mullins had happened upon his apparent treasure trove the night before. Moments later, the search party literally stumbled on John Mullins' head. Sticking up from the sand, Mullins' head— bloodied and dirty—seemed to be unattached to a body. Immediately, the worst was feared: poor Mr. Mullins had met some devilish strangers and had been brutally decapitated. But an inspection by the braver souls of the party revealed that Mullins was actually alive and that, as is always the case with a living person, his head was still very much attached to his body. Unfortunately, while his life had been spared, parts of his body had not. Both his ears had been sliced off.

It took some time to dig Mullins' battered body out of the sand. In the process, the party found a small bag of gold and silver coins tied around his neck. The strangers encountered the night before had forced Mullins to dig his own hole. In exchange for digging his own cell, Mullins had been rewarded with the coins from the treasure trove as payment, just as he had been promised. He was then thrown in the pit and buried, after which his ears were cut off.

The days that followed involved much panic in the Liverpool area, once Mullins' sickening story of privateers, plunder and precision slicing spread through the town. By late October 1782, in order to cull wild rumours and fears and to discourage piracy in the waters along the south shore, the government of Nova Scotia issued a reward of 20 pounds for the capture of the persons responsible for taking Mullins' ears. But, despite the modest reward, no one ever stepped forward to claim the money, and the men responsible for the mutilation disappeared with an unknown bounty, and identity, into the fog of history.

One December Night

Back in 1904, a strange occurrence took place in a Prince Edward Island farmhouse on a December night. Whether it was a forerunner of death, performed by some eerie ghost crackling in that dark foreboding night, or something else remains a mystery. Allan MacRae shares a story he found from a column titled "Legends of PEI" by Uncle Joe that appeared in the December 16, 1948 issue of *The Charlottetown Guardian*. He insists this is a true story.

On that December night, a light snow covered the ground outside. Inside, a little girl lay dangerously sick—so ill that her doctors said she might slip away any moment. For many days, members of her family had stood watch at her bedside. And when kind neighbours offered to relieve them, their offer was accepted with thanks and gratitude. The three were mature married women with families of their own, not the sort of people to get panicky over trifles. Certainly they were not superstitious.

By 10:00 PM, all members of the home were fast asleep. How they needed rest! The sick child lay in an adjoining room. Her mother lay beside her. All was peaceful and quiet. The only duty assigned the watchers was that of keeping the fires going and administering the medicines. They talked in lowered tones. At exactly five minutes before midnight, two of the three women started for the sick room. The people on the beds slept on, and the house was wrapped in silence. When they reentered the kitchen, the clock began striking the midnight hour.

Suddenly, a terrific, awful noise fell upon their ears, a noise that none of them could ever rightly define. Certainly, it was a new experience in their lives and one which they would never forget. It was like a mad rushing of waters after a spring thaw, or like the roaring of flames sweeping through dry timberland. Moments later, they heard a series of crackling sounds that seemed to come from within the building itself. The whole place rocked gently on its foundations, and the walls groaned and then appeared to expand and contract at frequent intervals. Thoroughly alarmed and shaking with fear, the watchers stood close together. Not a word passed among them. They just stood there and waited. Then all became as silent as ever.

After a time, courage came to them again, and they opened the door leading to the outside. Neither man nor beast was to be seen. Had anyone been snooping about, their tracks would have shown plainly in the fresh snow. The night was calm. The women finally agreed that they had heard a foreshadowing of the girl's death.

Entering the sick chamber, they found mother and child still asleep. The medicine was administered without even mentioning what had been heard. The little girl appeared to be growing weaker. Returning to the kitchen, the three settled down in their chairs to await the grim reaper. They were all quite sure the end would not long be delayed. The clock struck one o'clock.

The terrible, bloodcurdling noise again shook the watchers to their very bones. It was much like the first crackling, only many times louder. The kitchen door creaked on its hinges and then partly opened, though the night was perfectly calm. The experience was a bit too much for anyone

The Poker Face

As it is throughout the Maritimes, card playing is a tradi-
tional pastime in many Prince Edward Island communities
during the long winter months when darkness comes early.
Our pioneers brought card games with them from the Old
Country, and many games have survived to the present. But
what would a good card game be without covetous eyes,
a drink of rum and a bit of cheating? Researcher Allan
MacRae shares a story he found from a column titled
"Legends of PEI" by a mysterious writer known only as Uncle
Joe. The item first appeared in the December 28, 1948 issue
of *The Charlottetown Guardian*. According to Allan, this
poker game took place long, long ago in the community of
Rustico.

It used to be an old saying that a pack of cards was the
devil's prayer book. Another saying is that drink and cards
don't mix...and cheaters will end up with nothing...

Surely the two did not mix well that night, when a group
of Frenchmen were playing poker in a certain home in
Rustico. Rum and cards were being mixed freely that event-
ful night—or rather, that morning, for the old grandfather
clock that stood in one corner of the room pointed its hands
at 3:00 AM. John Barleycorn (the rum) did his level best to
keep the hearts of winners and losers in high spirits. The
game went on and on. Drink after drink was passed around.
On the table lay a considerable amount of money. The players looked at each other, trying, if possible, to read the hands
held by their opponents. All looked upon the money with
covetous eyes. Loud conversation, much of it fighting talk,

passed among the men as one or another of the group was caught cheating. It was quite obvious to everyone present that things were beginning to shape up badly.

A new hand just had been dealt, and the men were arranging the cards with deft fingers while bleary eyes looked this way and that, mistrust in every glance. Suddenly, up jumped one of the players, but the words of accusation he was about to utter died on his lips. He dropped back into his chair—silent, like a man who had been shot through the heart.

Under the table could be heard the rattling of chains, followed by a long, hollow laugh. The men around the table stiffened. The hands holding the cards began to tremble visibly. Fear played like a shadow upon their rough, unshaven faces. Their eyes opened wide as they tried to shake the effects of the potent liquor from clouded brains.

Then by some mysterious agent, the candles were snuffed out, leaving the room in semi-darkness. From under the table crept a figure. The chains rattled louder as the thing began to circle about the room. Not a man among them moved a muscle. Not a word was spoken. By now most of them were thoroughly sobered.

The crawling figure rose to a standing position. All eyes instantly focused upon it. They could see it better now: its cloven hoofs, the red hood upon its head, the long, two-tined fork held firmly in a pair of hairy, sinewy hands. The form moved again, lifted a long slender tail and wound it about its half-nude body. The mouth of the creature stood open in a horrible grin.

More magic! Both cards and money were snatched from the table by unseen hands. The silence of that room was the silence of the grave. Then from the mouth of the creature came a flame which left a slight odour of sulphur. Another horrible grin spread across the monster's face as it took a long, withering look at the terrified group. Then the door opened and the strange thing stepped across its threshold and vanished into the grey dawn of the morning.

*   *   *

In the Maritimes

• Seeing one crow means sorrow, two crows joy, three crows a letter, four crows a baby boy.

• Drinking water and looking into a mirror at midnight allows you to see the Devil.

5

Premonitions, Forerunners and Messages from Beyond

Lucy's Vision

In simple terms, a premonition is a foretelling of the future. Many people experience premonitions in everyday life, although skeptics say premonitions can be attributed to mere coincidence. You may experience them. The phone rings and you know who is calling, although the call was unexpected; you have a feeling that a specific song is going to play on the radio, and it does; you think of someone you haven't seen or heard from in a while, and they suddenly show up at your home for an unannounced visit.

Sometimes, premonitions aren't as specific, but they are just as strong, if not stronger. You have a nagging, undying feeling that something terrible is going to happen, and to one degree or another, it does. For instance, a great, unexplained feeling of sadness has been bothering you all day. You later learn that a close relative has died.

There are times, however, when a premonition is so strong that there is little doubt that the events as told in the vision are going to happen. These powerful premonitions are much rarer, but happen often enough that many researchers believe they are real. Some people seem to be more sensitive to these types of feelings, and they are called "sensitives" or "psychics." Research has shown these feelings are most powerful between close relatives, where the psychic bond appears the strongest.

Premonitions can be as subtle as a gnawing feeling or can be so overwhelming that they jolt you out of your everyday routine and prevent you from thinking of little else. They can be vague, nothing more than a feeling, or they can be so vivid that some people say it is like watching a film. Premonitions can foretell something that happens a minute, weeks or even many months later. They can come while you're doing something as mundane as washing the dishes, or they can come in dreams. Regardless, they often leave you with a void or empty feeling that something tragic is about to happen.

Lucy MacIntosh, from the picturesque island of Cape Breton, knows all too well what it means to see into the future. She's experienced it for herself. With a strong Celtic background and the Scottish family roots that run deep in Cape Breton culture, Lucy and her siblings are close. As the second oldest, she grew up keeping a close watch over her three younger brothers and younger sister. And as the six MacIntosh children grew into adults and began pursuing their own lives, with their own families and jobs that took them abroad, Lucy still kept close tabs on the clan, celebrating their successes and sharing their sadness. She was the glue that kept the family together.

Cameron, the youngest MacIntosh child, held a special place in Lucy's heart. He was an excellent student in school and an outstanding athlete, and Lucy and the other members of the MacIntosh family beamed with pride in 1989 when their baby brother went off to university, the only one in their immediate family to do so. He was destined for greatness, they believed. They all knew Cameron could achieve anything he wanted when he set his mind to it.

Leaving home is never easy for a young man or woman, but Cameron was determined to make the most of his opportunity. Heading off to university in Ontario with plans to first pursue a degree in business and then to study law and become a criminal lawyer, Cameron understood that he was leaving behind a family that loved him dearly. He also knew that if, for some reason, things didn't work out for him in Ontario, he could always return and they would welcome him with open arms. There would be no words of disappointment, only praise and encouragement for him to follow his own life path. But Cameron worked hard, and he was a success in university.

It was during Cameron's second year in Ontario that Lucy began experiencing deep feelings of sadness and sorrow that she could not explain. She felt them for several months starting in September; it was like something inside was warning her that a tragedy was about to befall the family. "I couldn't explain it," Lucy says. "It was just like I had this little voice inside my head whispering and telling me that something terrible was going to happen. I didn't know when, or to who it was going to happen, but I just had this terrible feeling every day for many weeks that something bad was going to happen to someone very close to me."

Then, one night in December 1990, Lucy's worst nightmares became reality. That's when she knew that those feelings she had been experiencing in the weeks leading up to that dreadful night were more than just her imagination. They were a warning.

Lucy recalls that it was a bitterly cold winter night. The family was busy preparing for the holidays, and everyone was anxious for Cameron's return. They hadn't seen him since late August when he drove to Ontario to start a new semester, and they missed him so very much. But even in the midst of all the excitement, Lucy could not shake a deep feeling of dread that something was not right. In her heart, she knew these feelings were not good. After all, she had grown up on Cape Breton Island, a place steeped in superstition and mystery.

On December 12, she went to bed around 10 o'clock. Her three daughters were sleeping, and her husband, Richard, was working late, so she seized the opportunity to catch up on her rest. She had not been sleeping well the last few weeks, and she was exhausted. Despite fits of restlessness leading to lots of tossing and turning, after about 45 minutes, Lucy fell fast asleep. Three hours later, she awoke with a start.

Richard, who had arrived home around 11 o'clock and had gone straight to bed, jumped quickly to his feet, thinking his wife was ill. Lucy was distraught, sobbing uncontrollably. She was shaking with such force that the entire bed was vibrating. She was nearly hysterical, trembling from head to toe. Through her tears, she told her disbelieving husband about her dream, but she insisted that she knew it was more than a dream. She told him she knew it was a premonition and that Cameron was not going to make it home for Christmas because by then he would be dead.

Trying to reassure Lucy that she had just had a nightmare, her husband offered to fix her some tea, the widely accepted remedy for whatever ails you. Insisting that it was more than a dream, Lucy told her husband that what she had seen was like a vision into the future. It was evening and very dark, she told him. It had been snowing, so the roads were slippery. Cameron had been on his way back from class when he lost control of his car, skidded across the yellow line and hit an approaching truck head-on. He was killed instantly. "He didn't have a chance," Lucy sobbed. "He didn't even know what hit him."

Contrary to reassurances from Richard that her baby brother was alive and well and despite the late hour, Lucy went straight to the phone and called Cameron. Finally, after six or seven rings, the groggy young MacIntosh sibling picked up the phone. "Hello, Lucy," he answered, knowing that only his older sister would phone at that time of night.

Thankful that her brother was okay, Lucy told him about her premonition. She knew that he would think she was crazy, but she made him promise that he would stay off the roads after supper the following night.

Wanting to get his emotionally distraught sister off the phone so he could go back to sleep, Cameron told her would try. He reassured her that he would take the bus. Then, after he told her how much he loved her, he hung up and went back to sleep.

But Lucy didn't sleep anymore that night. She felt her premonition was not a good sign. Throughout the next day and into the evening, Lucy was restless. She tried to reach Cameron many times by phone, but had no luck. By 11 o'clock, she knew something was not right. Her brother should have been home by now. She should be able to reach him.

Just before midnight, the phone rang and her husband answered. Lucy became hysterical. The call lasted no more than a minute. Hanging up the phone, her husband quietly confirmed her worst nightmare. The call had been from the Ontario Provincial Police Department. There had been a terrible car crash, and Cameron had been killed. They believe he died instantly when the car he was driving hit an approaching truck, just like in her dream.

A Special Gift

Can some people talk with the deceased, see dead people or foretell the future? Can they sense when disaster is about to strike or when a loved one is about to die? Can they see a tragedy before it happens? Many believe that some people possess such powers, a sixth sense, if you will. Pam Foley, who lives with her husband, Brian, in a rustic home in Milton, just outside Liverpool, believes some members of her family have such abilities. You be the judge.

Pam gained her fascination with the paranormal from her mother, Gala Manthorne. "My mom never believed in ghosts, but she did believe in forerunners, which were more acceptable because they authenticated local superstitions."

Gala was born in 1935 and lived around Liverpool her entire life. Pam recalls the stories as related by her mother. "When she was a young girl, she remembers sitting with her family one evening when her father's hat fell off a hook on the wall," Pam remembers. "He had been away, working in the woods. My grandmother looked up from her needlework and said, 'Your father's just been hurt.' Sure enough, he arrived home the next day with a broken leg."

Coincidence? Maybe, but Pam says there's more. "When my grandmother was in the hospital with cancer, the day she died, my mother had two experiences, almost simultaneously. She was on her knees, scrubbing the floor. Suddenly, she heard her name called out. When she turned to answer, she saw there was no one at the door. At the very same moment, a bird flew into the house."

In the Maritimes, we call these forerunners, tokens or omens. They are considered a foreshadowing of some tragic event, usually involving a family member or a close friend.

"Mom knew this was a bad omen," Pam continues. "A while later, she received word her mom had passed away."

Another coincidence? Pam doesn't think so. And that's not the end of it. "In 1976, on a Sunday, my father, Allen Manthorne, suffered a stroke and was in hospital in Halifax, recovering from his ordeal. My mother was taken to his sister's house in the city to stay. A few days later, a Wednesday evening, they received word that he had eaten a nice meal and was resting comfortably. Everyone felt better at the news. Mom had bedded down for the night, prepared to visit the hospital again the next morning. She was almost asleep when she awakened to see a shadow enter her bedroom. It was the size of a man, but didn't have any particular form or features. It settled itself at the foot of Mom's bed. She could feel the weight against her legs. It seemed to watch her for a while. Later that same night, the hospital phoned to say Dad had taken a turn for the worse."

Allen was dead before his family got to the hospital. He was 42. "Mom always believed this was my father's way of trying to see her one more time, and to let her know what was happening." More coincidence, or the hallucinations of an emotional woman worrying about her sick husband? Could Gala have had a sixth sense?

Pam believes her mother had the gift, and she recalls yet another story involving Gala's experience. "Another time, in the early 1990s, Mom was travelling with her companion down some deserted hauling roads in the woods, in his truck, in January, in the bitter cold. The truck broke down and, realizing they might die if they remained there in the cold, her companion set out on foot to get help. Mom expected he'd be right back, so she stayed behind and waited for help to arrive. She waited a long time. Eventually, she too set out on foot, thinking maybe her friend was in trouble. Fatigue and cold got to her, and she collapsed beneath a tree. As she sat there freezing, she started to feel warm and sleepy. Just as she was nodding off, a lady wearing a long black skirt arrived and kept her awake until eventually her friend arrived with help. Just as quickly as the mysterious woman appeared, she disappeared. Mom never saw a face, and she hadn't a clue about who the lady could have been, but she believed the woman saved her life."

Pam's mother died of cancer in 1993, but not before experiencing yet another unexplained phenomenon. "One evening, near the end, she lay awake in pain, wishing for some relief," Pam explains. "She was thankful to feel someone crawl in bed with her and hold her in their arms through the night so she could get some sleep. She was living with my family at the time, and commented the next morning that she really needed that special touch through the night. None of us had spent the night with her, but I always believed something special happened to Mom that night."

Did Gala have a guardian angel or was she just overly superstitious? It's hard to say, but it is clear through all of these stories that she seemed to be tuned in to a realm outside of what most of us consider normal. Perhaps these things can be explained, but sometimes it's better to suspend logic. Sometimes it's more fun to believe.

Duke Had a Message for Bessie

Forerunners come in a variety of sizes and shapes. They can take the form of human beings or animals. And they come without warning.

Bessie MacKenzie, who lives in Charlottetown, Prince Edward Island, the birthplace of Confederation, says without hesitation that she believes in forerunners, insisting that she has seen many of them in her 87 years. "My parents came from the Old Country," Bessie begins. "They believed in such things over there, and when they moved here, they brought those beliefs with them."

Some people—the skeptics—call her beliefs superstition, but she is indifferent to their cynicism. "I know what I know," Bessie says. "I've seen what I've seen, and I've seen a lot of strange things over the years. These are things that you can't simply explain because there is just no explanation."

When Bessie's mother died in 1971, she recalls that a bird hit their family home three days before she passed. "I expected her to die. She had been sick for some time, and when that bird hit the window, I knew it was her time. It upset me, but I wasn't surprised."

When her brother died in a car accident in 1974, three years after her mother's death, Bessie knew that he was going to be killed as well. "I saw him before he died just as sure as I'm talking to you right now. It was night and very dark and foggy, but I saw him come up the front walkway to our house and then, just like that, he disappeared. I knew it was his forerunner because it couldn't have been him. He was living in New Brunswick at the time. I knew there was no way he could be in Charlottetown. A couple days later, we got word that he had been killed in a terrible car accident."

When her father died in 1982, she was ready for that too. "I was sitting in my living room, rocking and knitting like I do every night, when the picture of Mom and Dad I had hanging in the dining room fell off the wall. For no reason, it just fell down. A couple minutes later, I heard three knocks at the back door, but when I went to check, there was nobody there. I knew it was my father letting me know that he was okay, that he had gone to be with my mother."

One of the saddest forerunners occurred in 1999 when she heard a baby crying in the upstairs bedroom of the house that she had shared with her husband for so long. The fact that she was alone when she heard the cries caused her great grief because she knew it was a sign that something terrible was about to happen. Her youngest daughter was pregnant then and living in Ottawa. The next day, Bessie received word from her son-in-law that her daughter had miscarried, and they had lost the baby. "I wasn't surprised," Bessie says matter-of-factly. "When I heard that baby cry the night before, I knew it was going to be bad news."

Over the years, Bessie has experienced many forerunners. They come to her without warning because they know she believes in them. "Why would they come to you if you don't believe?" she laughs. It's difficult talking about forerunners because of the sadness that surrounds each experience. "It always means death to someone I love, and it always leaves my heart broken," she says.

Her most difficult encounter with a forerunner surrounded the death of her husband, Ralph. The couple had been married for 56 years and she still misses him to this day, although he has been gone for many years. "It's hard to let go of someone after you've been together for that long," she says.

Bessie and Ralph met while she was a young teacher just out of college. He was a lobster fisherman working with his father until the licence became his. They had five children, and today, Bessie has 17 grandchildren, three great-grandchildren and one great-great-grandchild. Fiercely independent, she lives alone and insists that her family will never see her in a nursing home. "It's just not for me," she says.

When Ralph was diagnosed with lung cancer, the couple braced for a trying time. Doctors told them that the prognosis was not good and that Ralph might have only a year to live. "It's a hard thing to hear a doctor tell you that someone you love has only a year to live," Bessie recalls, the emotion in her voice betraying her feelings. Despite the strong façade this elderly woman puts forward, she still grieves for those she has lost. No amount of time can steel anyone to the point that they would become immune to such loss.

"Ralph went through a lot that year," she says. "As the time went by he grew more ill, and by the end, he was in a great deal of pain. At first, we tried to keep him home, but after a while it became too much for us to handle. It's hard to watch someone you love slowly slipping away."

About a month before Ralph died, their doctor finally insisted that he be admitted to hospital, both for his sake and for the well-being of Bessie. The doctor knew that working herself ragged taking care of her husband would not be healthy for the elderly woman. "It wasn't easy, but I finally agreed," Bessie says, but quickly points out that she spent every day with Ralph. Every morning, she made one of her children drive her to hospital by 9:00 AM. She would remain there, at his side, until 8:30 PM. She kept up this routine for several weeks.

One night, she had a visitor. It was shortly after nine o'clock when she finally sat down in her chair to do a bit of knitting before turning in for the night. After spending the day in the hospital with Ralph, she was exhausted, but her mind was racing so quickly that she could not make herself go to bed. "I had just made myself a cup of tea and settled down with my knitting when I heard the dog whining and scratching just outside the front door," Bessie recalls.

The sound of the dog at her front door unnerved her. Peeking outside, she could see no sign of the animal, but she knew what she had heard. "It was there. I had heard that sound many times in the past," she says.

Many years earlier, Ralph had a dog that would follow him everywhere he went. "Duke wasn't much more than a mutt—a mixed breed—but he was a good dog. Ralph and Duke were especially close. We loved him very much, and he was part of the family. That old mutt was with us for a lot of years. It was a sad day when Duke died."

On this evening, with her husband in hospital clinging to life, Bessie knew this wasn't a good sign. About 15 minutes later, her oldest son, Murray, arrived at her home. She knew right away it was bad news. "He told me the hospital had just called and that his father had just passed away."

"When?" Bessie asked her son.

"About 15 minutes ago," he answered.

But Bessie already knew. Duke had come to tell her that Ralph was now with him and that he was okay, that the pain was gone. "They were together again," Bessie says. And while she misses him every day, she knows he has gone to a better place.

Strange but True Stories

Some people seem to have an affinity to the paranormal. One such person appears to be Dave Conrad, a former resident of the Maritimes who, like so many others, moved away several years ago but still considers himself an easterner at heart. Dave now lives in Sidney on Vancouver Island. He left Liverpool in 1967 and worked in Dartmouth for a year before joining the Air Force. In 1974, he joined the Coast Guard, and he retired in 2003. He maintains close ties with his family back in Nova Scotia.

"My first experience with an apparition came when I was quite young, but I remember it vividly and will so to the end of my days," Dave begins. "Luckily, it was also one of the most beautiful things I have ever seen in my life."

Dave points out that he has an excellent memory of things from his youth. "I was about five or six and was playing outside with my older sister, Yvonne, and the Parnell brothers from next door. Suddenly, one of the Parnell boys said, 'What's that?' and we all looked to see a tiny human figure floating in the sky not far from us. It hung over the lake, and it appeared to be gazing directly at us. It was very close, and I remember it to be about 10 inches or a foot high, with very distinct human features. It was incredibly beautiful as it shone a very bright golden colour."

He recalls that it hardly moved for at least five minutes. "My sister, Yvonne, who was about 10, ran into our house and said, 'Mom, Mom, you have to come see the angel!' And our mother, who was also a witness to it, came running. It hung there in the sky for what seemed like ages, just shining its beautiful golden colour and looking at us. There was absolutely no fear in any of us. It finally disappeared and is now nothing but a beautiful memory for all of us who witnessed it."

When Dave thinks back to that experience, he wonders if what they saw that day so many years ago may have actually been the spirit of their grandmother who had recently passed away. "I don't know, but I would dearly love to see it again."

Relating his next brush with the paranormal, Dave beings, "My Aunt Eleanor told me about the death of our grandfather, Captain James Owen Conrad. He died in Halifax hospital. At the time, my grandmother, Ethel Conrad, was in Halifax at his bedside while my Aunt Eleanor babysat her brothers and sisters in the family home in Liverpool. For some curious reason, even his own children called our grandfather Captain Jim. On the evening that he died, Aunt Eleanor heard the distinctive thump of our grandfather's limp and the cane that he used coming down the very steep stairs. She knew it so well that it was unmistakable. She knew her dad was very, very ill but thought that somehow he had managed to come home. She ran to the stairs crying, 'Captain Jim, Captain Jim!' The distinctive thump of Grandad's heavy step and cane continued until it reached the bottom step, and then there was nothing."

When his grandmother returned from Halifax, Dave says they learned that his grandfather had passed away at the same time that his aunt had heard the sounds on the steps.

Another incident revolves around the death of Dave's father. "My dad died at home at the age of 37 from cancer," Dave recalls. "The end of his suffering in his last days was a blessing because of the terrible pain he went through.

Years later, my mother finally told me about an evening just after his death."

His mother had smoked the occasional cigarette and was doing so on that evening while looking out over the small lake near where they lived. Suddenly, she heard a hissing noise and looked toward the barn in the direction it was coming from. "She said she saw a small ball of white fire fly from the barn. It was hissing, and it went directly in front of Mom's face. It did a 90 degree turn at the corner of our house, then disappeared. I have heard that these are common apparitions that people believe are the dead letting the living know that all is well and that there is life after death. I personally believe this is was a message from Dad."

Dave's aunt also experienced something extraordinary when her brother died. "Our dad's sister, Evelyn, who now lives in a small town in Connecticut, woke up one night to find my oldest sister, Judy, kneeling in front of her bed praying. It was on the night that our dad died that she saw Judy, even though they were miles apart."

Because Judy was at home in Liverpool at the time, Evelyn took this to be a sign. She knew that her brother was very ill, and Judy's appearance so far away in another country told her of her brother's passing. "When Aunt Evelyn called home she said, 'Vernon died, didn't he.' He had. She then told my Mom what she had seen. Judy had been praying for Dad, and Aunt Evelyn, who had not seen any of us for so many years, even described over the phone exactly what Judy was wearing at the time."

Dave knows that while these occurrences may seem too extraordinary to be true, he insists they happened.

Grandmother's Rocking Chair

With a population of less than 1500, Souris is a small, rustic town in northeastern Prince Edward Island. Situated in an area famous for its beaches, the town is often referred to as the "Gateway to Basin Head." Souris started as a fishing village founded by the Acadians in 1727 and gradually grew to become the largest town on the eastern end of the island. Souris was infested by several mice plagues in the 18th century, and the town is named after the French word for mouse. The economy of the area is fueled by resource-based industries, mostly farming and the fisheries. And, with these industries facing an uncertain future, the region has turned to tourism, a sector that is growing quickly.

It is in the Souris area where one woman has struggled with the possibility that there is more to this life than meets the eye, or more specifically, more to the "other" life than we sometimes care to admit. Molly has requested that her identity not be revealed for fear of ridicule from those who do not believe in the afterlife. She fears that her family may be singled out because of their experiences, but she insists everything she is about to share is true. She asks people not to judge her story harshly or to dismiss her experiences, but instead to keep an open mind and try to believe that things can happen that defy logical explanation.

Molly says that to understand her story, it is important for people to know that as a child, she was very close to her maternal grandmother. "In fact, my grandmother was more like a second mother to me than a grandmother," she begins, a distinct hint of sadness and sorrow breaking through her otherwise strong facade. "We were very, very close, and I shared everything with her. The great thing about Nanny—that's what I called her—is that she would never react in a negative way. Even when I did something that I ought not to have done, she was stern but never angry with me. As I got older and shared more of my experiences with her, she would nod her approval for things she supported, or if she disagreed with something I'd done, she would give me the silent treatment. Not in a mean way, but to let me know that maybe I might want to give things a second thought. I don't think she had a mean bone in her body. She was very wise and thoughtful."

When her grandmother died in 1986, Molly, then in her mid-20s, took it hard. "It was one of the most difficult times in my life. Nanny had taken sick a few years before she died, and I spent a lot of time with her. When I wasn't working, I'd be with her. The family knew she didn't have much time left, and I wanted to make sure that I was with her right up to end, and I'm glad I was. It was hard, but I will cherish those times forever. We grew even closer in those last few months than even I thought was possible."

Near the end, as her grandmother's condition worsened, Molly spent many hours at her bedside. "She would not go to the hospital. She wanted to spend whatever time she had left in her own home and in her own bed. I understood that, but some of the family thought she should be in the hospital where the nurses could take care of her. But I knew none of that mattered to Nanny. She wanted to be in her house around the things she knew. Why deprive someone of that in the last days of their life?"

With her grandmother confined to her bed, Molly remained by her side, sitting in a rocking chair that her grandmother had kept in her bedroom for as long as she could remember. The older woman had explained that her own grandfather had made the rocking chair, and whenever anything happened to her, she wanted to make sure it remained in the family. Molly's grandmother told her the chair would be hers if she promised she would never part with it. "And of course I wouldn't. Why would I do that? I knew the chair was special to Nanny, and I promised I would keep it forever and pass it down to my own children and grandchildren, should I be fortunate enough to have a family. Nanny always laughed at me when I said things like that. 'Chin up, Molly,' she'd say. 'Of course you will have your own children. Why wouldn't you?'" Eventually, Molly did marry and had three lovely children of her own.

Molly remembers very well the night her grandmother succumbed to cancer after a brave two-year battle. It was shortly after 10 o'clock on February 16, 1986. "She was in a lot of pain in the end. She had been suffering for days and it was hard to watch, but in the last few minutes before she died, it was just like the pain all went away. I was really glad I was there. It made me feel better because I could see for myself that she went peacefully. She just stopped moaning, opened her eyes and stared off into the distance like she was looking at something or someone. Then she squeezed my hand—not hard, but just enough to let me know that she knew I was there with her—then she just closed her eyes and she was gone. It was as if she drifted peacefully off to sleep. It was hard to watch because I knew she was gone, but in a way, it was an amazing experience."

The days that followed her grandmother's death were hard for Molly. She had a hard time dealing with that loss. Her mother became increasingly concerned for her daughter's health because she would not eat, grew despondent and found it difficult to sleep. "It was hard for me. I missed Nanny so much. It was like there was a big hole in my heart, and I didn't think I'd ever get over it. In truth, I don't think you ever get over anything like that. Somehow, you just find a way to move on. You put the lost person on a shelf somewhere in your heart and keep them there until you need to remember them. When you need them, they're always there. That's how I think of Nanny. I find myself talking to her sometimes just like she's beside me." Pausing as if searching for the right words, Molly then adds, "And I know there are times when she is right beside me because I've seen her."

While she knows people will think that what she believes she has seen can be explained as an overactive imagination fueled by sorrow, Molly is convinced that her visions are real. The first time she saw her grandmother was two weeks after the older woman died. "It was late, maybe around one or two the morning. I had a hard time getting to sleep that night. I remember that, and it seems to me that I had just dozed off when I heard a sound that I had heard many times before. I knew what it was without even looking."

By this time, Molly's mother had agreed to allow her to move her grandmother's rocking chair into her bedroom. They thought that might somehow help her cope with the loss of her grandmother. "When I woke up that night, the first thing I heard was the creaking of the rocking chair as it rocked back and forth. It was very distinctive. There was no mistaking the sound."

Because Molly had been having trouble sleeping, her parents had started leaving a hallway light turned on at bedtime in the weeks since her grandmother's death. In the faint light that filtered into her room from the hallway, Molly could clearly see around her room. Glancing about, she was startled at first to discover her grandmother sitting in the rocking chair, slowly gliding back and forth. "It frightened me at first, I'll admit that," Molly explains. "I knew right away it was my grandmother's ghost, but I didn't scream or cry or anything like that. She looked nice, not like she looked before she died, but like she looked before she got sick. Her hair was pulled back, and she wore an ivory-coloured house dress like the kind she always wore. She looked really good. She looked healthy, not in any pain at all."

Slowly, as Molly lay in her bed watching her grandmother rock back and forth, she began to feel warm all over and, surprisingly, she began to relax. "I can't explain it. My grandmother didn't say anything, she didn't even look at me, but I felt like she was reaching out to me somehow. It was the oddest sensation. I just started to feel warm all over. I really didn't know what to do, so I just lay there watching the ghost of my grandmother as she rocked. She was there in my room that night even though she had died two weeks earlier." Molly isn't sure how long her grandmother remained there, but after a few minutes, she just seemed to fade away. And Molly began to drift to sleep.

In the morning, Molly felt better than she had since her grandmother's death. "I knew I hadn't been dreaming. I know my grandmother was there, and I think she came to bring me a message. I think she wanted to tell me that she was fine and that everything would be okay. I think she wanted me to know that no matter how bad things got, she'd always be here with me."

At first, Molly wasn't going to tell anyone about what happened, but later that day she confided in her mother about her grandmother's rocking chair. "My mother didn't say much, though. She just looked at me and told me to be very careful about what I tell people because someone might think I was crazy. I thought that was an odd thing to say, but I think my mother just wanted to protect me. I know some people can be cruel and mean with things like this, so while she didn't say if she believed me or not, she did want me to be mindful of how others would react. Come to think it, my mother has never come right out and said if she believed me or not."

In the years since her grandmother's death, Molly has seen the elderly woman on several other occasions. Years later, she saw her grandmother again sitting in the rocking chair two days before her father died. "That time, I think she was trying to prepare me for something terrible that was about to happen. My father had been sick on and off for a few years, but we really didn't expect him to die when he did. The doctors told us it was a massive heart attack and that he died instantly. After the shock wore off and I had time to think about things, I realized my grandmother had been trying to tell me something was going to happen. I hope he's there with her, wherever she is, because she always seems to be so peaceful. I want that for him."

On another occasion, Molly saw her grandmother one night during a terrible snowstorm when she was home alone. "That time, it was just a weird feeling. I was feeling very lonely and apprehensive. I'm not really sure if I was worried that something might happen, but I was in bed reading when I looked up, and there she was, just sitting there in the chair, rocking. She wasn't there for very long, just a few seconds, but I think she just wanted to let me know I wasn't alone."

And the last time she saw her grandmother was the night before her wedding. "I'll admit I was pretty nerved up about the wedding, and as I was fretting over the things I still had to do, there she was, suddenly, sitting in her rocking chair, rocking away, just as content as ever. That time I think she wanted to reassure me that I was going to be okay, that I would be happy, and I have been."

Molly hasn't seen her grandmother again since the night before her wedding, but she still feels her all around her just about every day. "Whenever I'm feeling down or a little stressed, I can sense her with me. I know she's there to guide me." In those times of stress, Molly finds the best way to calm her nerves is to sit in her grandmother's rocking chair and rock. "It's very relaxing and soothing. I now understand why Nanny wanted me to have it."

The Passenger in the Back Seat

Driving the highway between Moncton and Miramichi, the world-famous salmon fishing mecca located in northern New Brunswick, takes several hours. For the most part, the trek is long and tedious with many kilometres of nothing but forests and rocks to look at, and, if you're lucky, you might see the tail lights of a vehicle in front of you. If you're alone in your vehicle, it can be a particularly arduous trip. If it's late at night, it can also be extremely nerve wracking. And if you think you're alone in your car but it turns out you're not, it's even more disturbing. Shawn Baker, originally a Nova Scotian who now calls himself a New Brunswicker, recalls one night in summer 1995 when he all but ran off the road for fear of what he had just seen.

Shawn remembers that the region had been in the grips of an extended heat wave. It was a Sunday night, and he was travelling back to Miramichi, where he worked in the forestry industry. At that time he still often went home to Nova Scotia to visit. At least once a month, he'd head out from Miramichi after finishing work on Friday. It was always after six o'clock before he got away. He'd visit at home until Sunday night after supper, at which time he'd head north, hoping to get home by midnight so he could catch some sleep before work on Monday morning.

But on this particular day, Shawn had remained home until after nine o'clock because he was visiting family members he hadn't seen for many years and had decided to make the sacrifice of sleep. It was after one in the morning when he gunned his vehicle down the last stretch of highway heading toward Miramichi. And although he told himself he probably should have left much earlier than he had, he knew he had to stay awake if he was going to make it back in time to catch a few hours sleep. He needed the rest. It had been a fun weekend, but he hadn't gotten much sleep. He'd pay for it the next day if he went to work tired.

He was still two hours out of Miramichi when he began feeling so sleepy that he felt he should pull over to the road-side to catch a nap. An experienced driver, Shawn had never done this in the past. "I've spent thousands of hours on the road, and I don't ever remember when I've had to pull over and sleep."

But on this night, things were different. "I tried every-thing I could think of to keep awake. I had lots of coffee. I played the radio loud and I had the window rolled down to get lots of fresh air, but nothing was working. I was just too tired, and I could feel myself dozing off. I knew I had to get some sleep or I might have an accident."

Finding a wide section of open, straight highway, Shawn pulled his car over onto the shoulder of the road, turned off the ignition and closed his eyes. He dozed off immediately, but he wasn't asleep any more than maybe 10 or 15 minutes when he heard a man's voice. "No," he insists, "I wasn't dreaming. I know what I heard, and I positively heard a voice in my car that night. The deep voice was that of a man, and it simply said, 'Are you sure this is where you want to stop?'"

Quickly snapping to his senses, Shawn remembers look-ing in his rearview mirror and catching a fleeting glimpse of a man in the back seat of his car. "It was quick. He was there and then, in an instant, he was gone," Shawn says. "But he was there long enough for me to get a good enough look at him to know he was there, and I will never forget him."

The passenger in the back seat was middle-aged, maybe around 50, and he was heavy set, wearing a brown shirt. He had black hair and was sporting a moustache. "I remember him plain as day," Shawn says, adding that he immediately sprung awake after he heard the voice.

Jumping from the car, Shawn quickly opened all four doors and inspected the vehicle, both the front and the back. He thought someone had gotten in the car while he was asleep, but he found nothing. "Now, you might say my mind was playing tricks on me. I know I was pretty tired, but I swear there was a strange man in the back seat of my car one minute, and then he was gone. I can't explain it."

Once Shawn was sure there was no one else in the car, he turned on the ignition and resumed his trek back to Miramichi, now fully awake. "My heart was beating so fast and the adrenalin was flowing so quickly through my veins that I knew there was no longer any chance of me falling asleep again," he says. Two hours later, he made it home.

The next day, during his lunch break, Shawn was relaying his unusual experience to several of his co-workers, many of whom dismissed his claims that he had seen a ghost. They chided and kidded him, saying he was so exhausted from a weekend of partying that his mind was just playing tricks on him. But not everyone who heard his story was so quick to discount the tale.

"This was a man, you said?" a colleague asked Shawn.

"Yes, a man about 50 years of age, I'd say."

"And you say you saw him about two hours from here on a straight stretch of highway?" his co-worker continued.

"That's right. On the road from Moncton."

Shawn's friend then told him that 11 years earlier, a fatal motor vehicle accident had occurred in that exact spot involving five cars. The only fatality was a middle-aged man.

The revelation hit Shawn like a bullet. Had he seen the ghost of the man who died in that accident? Had the ghost been trying to warn Shawn that this part of the highway was not safe? I guess we'll never know for sure.

*   *   *

In the Maritimes

- Whistling on the deck of a boat brings on a storm.

- Red sky at night, sailors delight. Red sky in the morning, sailors take warning.

Experiences at the Cemetery

The Fundy Parkway, just outside the seaside village of St. Martins, an hour east of Saint John, has proven to be a great attraction for hikers and cyclists—and anyone interested in eerie experiences.

New Brunswick ghost chaser and writer David Goss says the eerie experiences are provided by Barbara McIntyre and Fay Marks. The original version of this story appeared in a column by David in the *Moncton Times & Transcript*. With advance notice, Barbara and Faye will take visitors off the beaten paths of the parkway and into the woodlands, where they have discovered two small family burial grounds. They have discovered these plots were used by the Fownes and Melvin families when they first settled the area in the 19th century.

The graveyards had been known by lumbering crews over the years but were largely forgotten by most residents of the area. However, Barbara says, "I felt that if people were going to be walking near them, something had to be done about these cemeteries. So, in April 2000, we located four tombstones in the Fownes cemetery and two in the Melvin cemetery and began working to upgrade them."

That is when they started to have some eerie experiences that seem to suggest that the dead buried there were not too happy with the way things had gone over the years, perhaps especially with the fact that the lumbermen had desecrated the sites with their regular cutting of the trees.

Barbara says, "One day I was there with another fellow named Charlie, and we had roped the Fownes area off with orange danger ribbon. Suddenly Charlie said, 'Oh my God!' I said, 'What's the matter Charlie?' He said, 'Look down there.' This was a day that was dead calm, yet the orange line marker for the edge of the cemetery was fluttering. I laughed, and said in teasing fashion, 'Oh, Charlie, we must have left someone's feet outside the fence.' So we measured again, changed the line, and the fluttering stopped."

She continues, "To find some bodies, we used a probe into the ground, and we were also going to use a young fellow in Black River who could find where people were buried by divining, like with water. There was a girl working at the museum who was interested in old cemeteries and wanted to help. Her name was Pam. She asked one day if she could go up with us. By then, we'd found about 35 plots. The stones weren't in the right places because bulldozers had come through years before. Pam walked all through both cemeteries. She never said a word. On the way home, I looked into the back seat. She was sitting there crying, tears rolling down her face. I asked her, 'What's the matter with you?' She said, 'I just get choked up in cemeteries. Most of the people in the cemetery are content, but some are not, and you haven't found all of them yet.'"

Barbara asked Pam if she thought she could find them. "She said that she'd like to try, and she later identified about 11 more sites.

"One day we moved some rocks that she said were out of place. When we did, she told me, 'There's a woman sitting on this rock and she's talking to a man in that grave.' I walked to the spot she was pointing to. It was covered in bushes, but I could feel an indentation. Pam said, 'She's buried here right beside him.' We cut away the bushes, and you could see both indentations beside the rock."

On another day, workmen were busy cutting away alder bushes with a bush saw and a whipper snipper. "Just before I got to the cemetery, I couldn't hear anything. When I got there, the men were just standing in the cemetery looking puzzled. I asked them what was wrong. They said that they had just gotten the equipment fixed, but it wouldn't work in the graveyard. But outside the graveyard, both fired right up. They walked inside the gate, and both the bush saw and the whipper snipper quit. That day, no work got done inside the fence." And on another day, Barbara's camera refused to work inside the cemetery, but worked fine outside.

"Pam revealed more information as time passed," Barbara says. "One instance was a claim that a mother was crying for her twin girls. Then one day she told us she sensed there were three children that had died of diphtheria, and they were buried in the graveyard. Later, not five feet away, a memorial stone was uncovered with three children's names on it."

Barbara was amazed each time Pam revealed new information. She notes, "We had cut a path to give us a circular route. Pam took off through the bushes one day, saying she felt it was the pathway to the house. She came out into a clearing and announced that the house was right ahead. She said the dead were not happy that another path had been cut, and we should let it grow in."

They continue to make discoveries and to have eerie experiences to this day.

Ghostly Glossary

ANGELS: Derived from the Greek word *angelos* ("messenger"), angels are the celestial messengers and guardians of a deity; though commonly associated with Christianity, angels are common to many religions. They are immaterial beings, sexless creatures of pure consciousness that possessed a knowledge no mortal could ever even hope to comprehend.

CLAIRAUDIENT: An individual with the ability to perceive sound or words beyond the range of hearing. These sounds can come from outside sources such as spirits or other entities. Clairaudience is said to be a form of channeling messages through audible thought patterns.

COLD SPOTS: Commonly associated with haunted sites, a cold spot is said to result from a ghost absorbing the necessary energy to materialize from its surroundings. They are usually quite localized and are 10 or more degrees cooler than the surrounding area.

DEMON: In Christian theology, demons are the instruments of evil, the fallen angels cast out of heaven with Lucifer. They exist for no other purpose but to torment and torture the living through abuse, assault and possession. However, in other cultures, demons are not nearly so malicious. To the Greeks, *daimons* (translated, the word means "divine power") served as intermediaries between mortals and the gods of Mount Olympus.

ECTOPLASM: A term popularized in the film *Ghostbusters*, ectoplasm is said to be a white, sticky, goo-like substance with a smell resembling ozone. It is, hypothetically, a dense bio-energy used by spirits to materialize as ghosts. Its existence has never been proven.

EMF: An electromagnetic field, or EMF, is associated with an electric charge in motion. Many paranormal researchers equate an EMF with paranormal activity, believing that ghosts generate high levels of electromagnetic energy through their activities.

ESP: Extrasensory Perception, or ESP, describes the ability to perceive and receive information without the use of any of the usual five senses: sight, touch, smell, hearing and taste. Not surprisingly, ESP is often referred to as the sixth sense.

EVP: Electronic Voice Phenomena, or EVP, is a process through which the voices of the dead are captured on an audiocassette. How the process works is a bit of a mystery, but it usually involves placing a tape recorder at a haunted site. When played back, the voices of the dead should be clear on the recording and should not be confused with background noise or static.

EXORCISM: An exorcism is the purging of a person, place or thing that has been possessed by a demon or other unnatural force. It is normally carried out under the close supervision of a religious official, thoroughly trained and capable.

GEIGER COUNTER: An instrument that detects and measures radio-activity, or the spontaneous emission of energy from certain elements. This device searches for fluctuations in Alpha, Beta, Gamma and X-ray radiation, which point to a disturbance in spirit energy.

GHOST: Derived from the German word *geist* and the Dutch word *geest*, a ghost is the physical manifestation of an individual's disembodied spirit. It may appear as a figure, but a ghost can also manifest itself through smells, sounds and other sensations. At the heart of any belief concerning ghosts is the idea of a separation between the physical body and the metaphysical soul. The body perishes, though the soul does not.

MATERIALIZATION: The process through which seemingly solid objects or individuals appear out of thin air. It was a popular and well-documented phenomenon during the earliest years of Spiritualism, when mediums commonly caused objects like coins and cups to materialize.

ORBS: Though they may vary in shape, colour and size, orbs are most commonly round in shape and whitish grey in colour and are usually, though not always, found in photographs taken during a haunting or at a haunted site. They are believed to represent the spirit of the dead. Because dust, moisture and lens flare can easily be confused with orbs, some critics have argued that orbs may not be enough proof to legiti-mize a haunting.

OUIJA BOARD: An instrument that allegedly can be used to contact or channel spirits of the deceased. It is usually a wooden or cardboard device inscribed with the alphabet, the words "yes" and "no" and the numbers 0 to 9. There is usually a slideable apparatus on rotating castors or wheels with a pointer. The operators of the board place their fingers lightly on the slideable device and wait for it to move.

PARANORMAL: Any event that cannot be explained or defined through accepted scientific knowledge is said to be beyond what is normal. It is, therefore, paranormal.

POLTERGEIST: A combination of two German words, *poltern* (to knock) and *geist* (spirit), a poltergeist is characterized by its bizarre and mischievous behaviour. Activities of a poltergeist include, but are not limited to, moving furniture, throwing objects and rapping and knocking on walls. A poltergeist may also be responsible for terrible odours and cries. Typically, the activities of a poltergeist appear unfocussed, pointless and completely random.

POSSESSION: A condition in which all of an individual's faculties fall under the control of an external force, such as a demon or deity. An individual possessed by a demon may alter his or her voice, even his or her appearance, and be fearful of religious symbols.

REVENANT: From the French *revenir* (to return), a revenant is a ghost that appears shortly after its physical death. Usually, it will only appear a few times, perhaps even just once, before disappearing from the earth forever.

THERMOGRAPH: A self-recording thermometer that traces temperature variations over time.

TRANCE: A trance is essentially an altered state of consciousness in which the individual, though not asleep, is barely aware of his or her immediate environment. There is some speculation that during a trance, the body enters a state that hovers somewhere between life and death, which frees the mind to explore a higher realm and gain spiritual insight.